Alan ... 922.
He l... his
fathe... ing on the
Norfolk B... the *Eastern*

The Inspector George Gently series

Gently Does It
Gently by the Shore
Gently Down the Stream
Landed Gently
Gently Through the Mill
Gently in the Sun
Gently with the Painters
Gently to the Summit
Gently Go Man
Gently Where the Roads Go
Gently Floating
Gently Sahib
Gently with the Ladies
Gently North-West
Gently Continental

Gently with the Ladies

Alan Hunter

Constable & Robinson Ltd
55–56 Russell Square
London WC1B 4HP
www.constablerobinson.com

First published in the UK by Cassell & Company Ltd, 1965

This paperback edition published by Robinson,
an imprint of Constable & Robinson Ltd, 2012

A copy of the British Library Cataloguing in
Publication Data is available from the British Library

ISBN: 978-1-78033-938-2 (paperback)
ISBN: 978-1-78033-939-9 (ebook)

Typeset by TW Typesetting, Plymouth, Devon

Printed and bound in the UK

1 3 5 7 9 10 8 6 4 2

For James Turner

CHAPTER ONE

'WHAT'S YOUR NAME?'

'Fazakerly.'

'John Sigismund Fazakerly?'

'Yes.'

Gently looked curiously at this man, for whom the police had been searching three days. In a penthouse flat in Chelsea his wife, Clytie Fazakerly, had been found battered to death, and the divisional C.I.D. had little doubt who had done it. And now here he'd walked into Gently's office, after waiting three hours down below: a shabby, tired, unkempt man, looking close to the end of his tether. 'Nobody we know,' desk had said on the phone. 'Won't give his name or his business. Do you want us to move him on, Chief?' And Gently had nearly grunted: 'Yes!'

Instead . . .

'You knew we were looking for you, Fazakerly?'

'Yes – at least, I do now.'

'What does that mean?'

'I didn't know till I saw a paper this morning.'

'Where have you been then?'

'Off-shore, mostly.' He made a weak motion with his hand. 'In a yacht I hired at Rochester. You can check with the owners. Bossoms.'

And in fact he was dressed in dirty slacks and an old sweater, over which he was wearing a reefer jacket on which the stains of salt showed. He had a two-day growth of beard on his fine-boned, sallow face, and a nasty abrasion across the forehead which he'd come by recently. A tall man. He kept shifting his weight from foot to foot as he stood. You had the feeling that if you nudged him he'd just fall down and lie where he fell.

'Take a seat.'

Fazakerly slumped into one. He sat resting his arms on his knees.

'Right,' Gently said. 'You've read the papers. You'll know pretty well where you stand.'

Fazakerly nodded. 'I know.'

'Then you won't be surprised at what I'm telling you. You're under arrest, and anything you say may be taken down and used in evidence.'

'Yes, I know about that.'

'As long as you do,' Gently said. 'Perhaps now you'll tell me why you're here. This case is nothing to do with me.'

Fazakerly closed his eyes. 'Because you're my only chance,' he said. 'Because I know you'll listen to me and maybe know I'm not lying.'

'We'll listen, don't worry,' Gently said. 'You'll have every chance to tell your story.'

'That's not enough. I can't prove enough.'

'Then how does it help coming to me?'

Fazakerly didn't reply at once, sat, eyes closed, leaning forward. He was all in, that was no act: around each eye was a bruise-like halo. And there was something familiar about him, something Gently couldn't directly place. Had he met him before? He remembered no Fazakerly, and the name was not one easily forgotten.

'You see . . . I know how you work. You're not just hell-bent to make a case. Oh, you can put on the heavy policeman stuff, but that isn't why you're at the top. No . . . you care about what happens, you want the truth, all the truth.'

'Thanks for the compliment, but it won't help you.'

'It will, it must. It's my only chance.'

'Then you'd best forget about it, Fazakerly. The case belongs to Q Division.'

'No, listen to me – please listen!'

'You're wasting my time. I'm a busy man.'

'If you just hand me over I'm a dead duck. For God's sake, give me this one chance!'

Gently hesitated, phone in hand. This wasn't the usual approach by any means. The quiver of entreaty in Fazakerly's voice had to be genuine. He stared at Fazakerly uncertainly.

'Look,' he said. 'You'll get a fair crack of the whip.'

'That isn't enough.'

'It is if you're innocent.'

'Please put that phone down. For five minutes.'

Gently looked at the phone. 'All right,' he said. He

banged the phone back on its rest. 'Now,' he said. 'Five minutes. But after that, you're in a cell.'

Fazakerly lit a cigarette with hands that trembled. They were blistered and dirty hands and several of the nails were broken. He took a long drag into his lungs and it seemed to perk him up at little. He looked Gently in the eye. He had light brown eyes with golden flecks in them.

'You nearly remember me, don't you?' he said.

If Gently felt a stab of surprise, it didn't show in his face.

'I'm not trying to make anything of it, but you'll understand better for knowing. I'm a distant relative of Geoffrey Kelling's. I was a guest at the wedding.'

So that was it! No wonder if Gently's memory had let him down. It was twenty-five years since his sister's wedding: Bridget had married the year war broke out.

'You're Geoffrey's relative?'

'A second cousin. I shook hands with you at the reception. I'm telling you this so you understand – I really do know how you work. I mean, you're famous, we're proud of the connexion, we read up your cases and trials. I didn't come here by accident. I knew only you could help me.'

Gently grunted. 'I'd sooner you'd come on a social visit,' he said.

'I'm sorry. I promise not to spread it around.'

'It wouldn't do you any good if you did.'

But it would, as Gently knew well: points were stretched for policemen's relatives. Where they were concerned you double-checked and bent over backwards to give fair play. What was more, Inspector Reynolds of Q Division was an admirer of Gently's, and the mere fact that Fazakerly had been to the great man would be a mark in his favour. Had Fazakerly guessed it, coming to Gently? No . . . that was too far-fetched.

'Could you stand a coffee?' he asked gruffly.

'My God, yes. I've had nothing since yesterday.'

'Why not?'

'I planned on having breakfast ashore. Then I saw the paper and grabbed the first train.'

'Where was this?'

'Harwich. I dropped my hook there at six this morning. You may not have noticed, but there's been a blow on. I've been damned near over to Holland and back.'

Gently rang down for coffee and sandwiches. His five-minute limit had already gone west. Fazakerly, sure now of Gently's attention, inhaled cigarette smoke for some moments. Then he said quietly:

'But of course, that's no alibi. I could have killed her before I left. That's the trouble: I'm wide open. Opportunity, motive, I've got everything. So I must have someone who believes in me, who can look at it from my point of view. Who'll take my word, that's about it. On the pure facts, I'm sunk.'

Gently hunched his shoulders glumly. 'So what are these pure facts,' he said. 'You quarrelled with your wife about another woman, you ran away, and she's found dead.'

'Yes.' Fazakerly closed his eyes. 'And don't forget Clytie's money. I'm a bum, a social parasite. I needed her money. That's the clincher.'

'Have you none of your own?'

'Not a sou. Except what I pick up round the studios. I'm a photographer, you know, or I was once, and sometimes they put a job in my way. And Clytie, of course . . . she made me an allowance. Oh, my character won't save me.'

'But you didn't kill her.'

'No. Everything else I admit. Yes, she'd found out about Sarah Johnson, yes, there was a row, yes, I ran. Straight to Sarah, straight to Rochester. I wanted Sarah to say, let her divorce you.'

'And Sarah didn't.'

Fazakerly nodded. 'Perhaps it was a bit too much to ask. Sarah doesn't have any money, and I'm just one big bloody liability. I stink, you know. I really do. I ought to have gone out there and got drowned.'

The messenger arrived with a tray, which he placed on the desk nearest to Fazakerly. He stared interestedly at Fazakerly while Gently initialled the receipt-book. After he'd gone Fazakerly said dully:

'I'll have to get used to that, won't I?'

'Eat your sandwiches!' Gently grunted.

Fazakerly shrugged and began to eat.

Gently smoked. It was only slowly that the implications of this business were becoming clear to him. Till a moment ago he was still seeing it as something he could toss straight back to the proper department. But was it so easy? From an official view, nothing else was required of him, in fact he'd be treading on people's toes if he stepped outside procedure. But there was Geoffrey and Bridget too: sometime he'd have to tell them what happened, and a plea of procedure would sound pretty thin when they learned that Fazakerly had come to him for help. Oh, they'd be understanding and nice about it, but still, they wouldn't be able to help wondering . . .

He watched resentfully while Fazakerly bolted the sandwiches and drank great gulps of steaming coffee. So he'd made a mess of things, this idle waster! But why did he have to drag Gently in too?

'Right,' he snapped. 'If you didn't kill her, perhaps you can tell me who did.'

Fazakerly shook his head, chewing on a sandwich. 'Not the faintest,' he mumbled, 'unless it was Sybil.'

'Who's Sybil?'

'Sybil Bannister. She's the bitch who lives in the flat below. But Sybil wouldn't want to kill Clytie. Me perhaps, but not Clytie.'

'Why you?'

Fazakerly swallowed some coffee. 'Because I was superfluous, don't you see? My God, you're not dealing with decent people, you're down in the depths, you're stirring ordure. I haven't been Clytie's husband for years, not since Sybil moved in. She's an old flame from Bristol. They were going strong together at school.'

'You mean, a Lesbian relationship?'

'Exactly. Clytie was always a bit that way. She looked as though butter wouldn't melt in her mouth, but that was all part of the act.'

'And this Sybil Bannister upset your marriage?'

'Let's say she gave it the last nudge. Clytie was fooling with girls before that. We never had much of a sex-life together.'

He tore a mouthful from another sandwich and washed it down with more coffee, then he grinned weakly at Gently.

'Tell me if I'm shocking you,' he said.

Gently made a face. 'So why did you marry her in the first place?' he asked.

'Oh, money.'

'Just that?'

'It's all the picture needs, isn't it? Actually, she had a torso too, and a sort of promising manner. Only it wasn't promising me anything. Though I didn't find that out till later.'

'Didn't you love her?'

'I've forgotten. Such a long time ago.'

'And it doesn't matter to you that she's dead.'

Fazakerly closed his eyes. 'Not much,' he said.

Then his eyes sprang open again. 'Look, I'm being truthful!' he exclaimed. 'I know I'm knocking nails in my coffin, but if I used whitewash you wouldn't believe me. I'm a bum, I've said it before. I've got the motives of a bum. The only decent thing left in me is down that river, out at sea. When I'm alone there, then I'm decent, I can look the sun in the face. But I'm a bum the rest of the time: a lousy bum: but not a murderer.'

'All right, calm down,' Gently said. 'Just don't give answers like that in court.'

'Do you think I'm stupid?'

Gently stared at him. 'No,' he said. 'You're far from stupid.'

Fazakerly went on eating and drinking, his eyes wide and distant.

'Yes,' he said, 'that's where I'm decent. That's where I should be all the time.'

Gently sighed and re-lit his pipe. 'Let's get back to pure facts,' he said. 'You went to the flat at about three p.m. on Monday. What were you doing before that?'

'I was at Rochester.'

'With this other woman?'

'Of course. I'm always there at weekends. I belong to the Cruising Club, you know? It's the only thing that keeps me sane.'

'So you'd just come back from a weekend with her when you went to the flat, and your wife had got to know about this, and there was a violent quarrel.'

Fazakerly nodded.

'How had she found out?'

'Some nice person told her, I daresay. I mean, I hadn't been terribly discreet, there'd never seemed any need for it. I'd played around a bit before. Clytie had never taken any notice. In fact, I was more surprised than anything when she started sounding off about Sarah.'

'Did she know Sarah?'

'No.'

'But she was emphatic you were to drop her.'

'Emphatic is right,' Fazakerly said ruefully. 'They don't come any more emphatic than Clytie.'

'And she'd have threatened you.'

'She did. I was to drop Sarah or else. Meaning my allowance would be cut off and I'd be kicked out of the flat. Imagine a bum hearing that sort of threat, and coming from another bum like Clytie – because, hell, where did her beautiful money come from? I'll tell you – from a step-uncle who used to lay her.'

'And that made you angry.'

'Are you kidding?'

'So angry that you picked up the nearest weapon.'

'But I tell you—'

'The weapon that has your fingerprints on it: and you hit your wife over the head.'

'Now look here—!'

'Isn't that how it happened? Why you were seen running down the stairs? Why you grabbed a yacht and set a course for Holland – until you remembered your connexion at the Yard?'

Fazakerly stared, mouth open, a sandwich trembling in his hand.

'This is a trap!' he cried. 'You've got people listening – a tape-recorder – you're trying to trap me!'

Gently shook his head. 'Oh no.'

'But I trusted you – I'm telling you everything.'

'Were you going to tell me about the murder weapon?'

'I don't know about that. I don't!'

'Where was your wife when you left her?'

'Where we had the row – in the lounge.'

'That's where she was found.'

'I can't help that!'

'And where the murder weapon was kept. Nobody else was seen to visit the flat, only your prints are on the weapon. For the second time I'm asking you – if you didn't kill her, who did?'

Fazakerly's mouth opened and closed, but no sound came out. A colour that had begun to return to his washed-out face vanished, leaving it a pasty grey.

'Well?'

He swallowed. 'You're trying it on – that's all you're doing, isn't it?'

'You think so?'

'Yes, a test. You want to see how I'll stand up.'

'I think you're guilty.'

'No you don't! You're testing me, seeing if I go to pieces. You know damned well it wasn't me, I'm not the type, I wouldn't kill anyone.'

'So why are your prints all over the weapon.'

'That's another try-on!'

'No it isn't.'

'Then it's something I've handled at another time – that's possible, isn't it? If it belongs in the flat?'

Gently looked at him, said nothing.

'Yes, it's something I've handled,' Fazakerly said. 'Something that would take a set of prints . . .' He stopped. 'Oh my God,' he said. 'Not that!'

'Not what?'

'Not the belaying-pin.'

Gently said flatly: 'The belaying-pin?'

'A trophy – a silver-plated belaying-pin – it hung on the wall in the lounge!'

'It did, did it,' Gently said.

Fazakerly's pale eyes fixed on him. For a moment there was no sound in the office, not even of two men breathing. Then Fazakerly's face seemed to crumple.

He said hoarsely: 'So that's it, isn't it? Not you nor anyone will believe me now, not if the weapon was my belaying-pin.' His eyes closed. 'Oh Christ,' he said, 'it's coming home. That poor bitch.'

Gently picked up the phone. 'I'm sorry,' he said. 'I have to do this.'

'I thought there was a chance,' Fazakerly said. 'I didn't know. It wasn't in the paper.'

'No, it wasn't,' Gently said, then he spoke into the phone. Fazakerly sat silently, his head in his hands, the abrasion livid on his pale forehead.

Gently hung up. 'Right,' he said. 'There's only one thing I can do for you. This chat of ours is off the record. You can start afresh with Inspector Reynolds.'

'But what's the point?'

Gently shrugged. 'You let your hair down with me. Maybe you've learned what not to say, it could be a little help.'

'But you're through with me, aren't you?'

'Did you expect anything different?'

'I didn't kill her. I thought if I saw you, if I could tell you, you'd know it was true.'

'I'm not psychic,' Gently said.

'Of course . . . but there must be a difference. Even with a lying bum like me, it must sound different when I'm telling the truth. When I've nothing to hide, when I'm right behind it, when I'm naked there with the fact. Something in my eyes, in my voice. God, there *has* to be a difference!'

'Perhaps you'll convince Inspector Reynolds.'

'But you – you can't tell?'

'No.'

'Then I'm sunk. Because being innocent is all I've got.'

He let his head sink into his hands again, but raised it again a moment later.

'Tell me,' he said. 'What shall I get . . . fourteen years, something like that?'

Gently sighed, but said nothing.

There was a knock on the door.

After they'd taken him away Gently strode over to the window and stood looking out at the yellowy Thames. A patrol boat coming up was making heavy weather against the brute force of the ebb. The dull sky of the past few days was still heavy over the city, but the boisterous wind of yesterday had fallen almost to a flat calm. Gently returned to his desk and picked up the phone.

'Put me through to Records.'

Ellis, the organizing brain of Records, was also a keen yachtsman.

'Hullo . . . Ellis?'

'Oh – Gently.'

'Look, I want some yachting information. If someone took a yacht out of Rochester last Monday p.m., would yesterday's wind have affected him much?'

'What moron did that?'

'Would he need to be a moron?'

'There were gale warnings out for the whole coast. He was either a moron or an intending suicide.'

'Well, he might have been an intending suicide,' Gently said. 'He was certainly under some stress. But either way, what would have happened after he'd sailed out of Rochester?'

'Just a minute, I'll do some homework.'

There was a rustling and squeaking at the other end. Then Ellis said:

'He couldn't have left Rochester much before half past six. By then it was blowing Force 6 from the sou'west, and soon it was gusting Force 8, and by midnight it was blowing a full gale, and it didn't ease for the next twenty hours.'

'What would he have done?'

'He might have put out a sea-anchor, and perhaps set a jib to keep him heading. He'd be just running before it, if that's what you mean, there'd be no chance of him steering a course.'

'Where would that take him?'

'Oh . . . the Hook. Perhaps higher up, Ijmuiden way.'

'Then, if he set a course back when the wind eased . . .'

'With a bit of luck he'd lay Harwich.'

Gently hung up and sat frowning. So Fazakerly was perhaps telling the truth about his sea-trip. But that proved nothing, as he admitted himself: he had no reason to lie about that. All the same . . .

He grabbed up the phone again.

'Get me Q Division, Inspector Reynolds.'

While he waited he snatched up a ball-pen and began sketching a belaying-pin on his blotter.

'Reynolds? Gently here. About Fazakerly.'

But first he had to endure Reynolds' congratulations. An earnest, moustached man from Battersea, he never missed a chance of paying Gently homage.

'Yes . . . well, I want to ask you a favour. It turns out he's connected with my in-laws. No, I think he's guilty too, but I feel I ought to make the motions . . . What I want is you don't charge him for the next twenty-four hours, right?'

Reynolds hesitated, and Gently could picture the consternation on his solemn, Saxon face.

'But if I don't charge him, Chief . . .'

'You'll be able to hold him. You'll need some time to check his story.'

'Are you taking over, then?'

'No, nothing of that sort. I'm just clearing my slate with the family. Please understand I'm not interfering, I'm only concerned with getting the facts.'

'Yes, of course, Chief. I'll do what you say.'

'Thanks. I'll drop round after lunch.'

Under the belaying-pin he printed in capitals:

WITH REMISSION, SAY NINE YEARS.

CHAPTER TWO

AT DIVISIONAL HEADQUARTERS in Chelsea Reynolds greeted Gently with anxious eyes. He shook hands respectfully, but his first words were:

'Chief, I'm afraid he's for the high jump.'

'Of course he is,' Gently shrugged.

He pushed into the C.I.D. man's office. Lying on Reynolds' desk, with a label tied to it, was the silver-plated belaying-pin. Gently hefted it curiously. It was probably an antique which had been prettied-up to make a trophy, and it was inscribed: 'Rochester Sail Cruising Club', with a list of names, ending: 'J. S. Fazakerly.'

'Which end would he have held?' Gently asked.

'Well, there was blood and some hair on the sharp end. It was kept in a bracket on the wall, so if you snatched it down you'd be holding the knob.'

'Would he have got some blood on himself?'

'Perhaps, but she was wearing a turban hair-style. He says the clothes he was wearing are in a locker at Rochester. I've sent down to fetch them and pick up his car.'

'His prints check?'

'Oh yes. They're identical with those we had from his gear. His right index finger matches the print on the weapon. I've some photographs here.'

He handed Gently a bunch of glossies which were still cockled and smelling of developer. Gently leafed through them quickly, pausing to stare only at one. He handed them back.

'Just one clear print – and the others partial and erased.'

'Do you think he tried to wipe them off?'

'He made a curious job of it if he did.'

'What do you think, then?'

Gently grunted. 'I know what his counsel will suggest we think – that someone wearing gloves handled the pin. Do you have any answer to that?'

Reynolds gazed at the photographs. 'Wait a minute,' he said. 'Yes – the housekeeper was wearing gloves. She was the one who found the body. She still had her gloves on when we got there.'

'And she'd handled the pin?'

'I'll bet she had.'

'But do you know it for a fact?'

Reynolds shook his head impatiently. 'I soon will do. I'll send Buttifant round to ask her.'

'Still,' Gently said, 'if she didn't, that's a point you'll have to watch. And while I'm playing the Devil's advocate, I'll just ask you something else. You'll have had a long session with Fazakerly?'

'Of course, Chief.'

'Did you let him smoke?'

Reynolds wriggled his shoulders. 'It's an open-and-shut case. I didn't see any need to be tough with him.'

'But did you notice anything?'

'Well . . . nothing special.'

'In the way he lit his fag, or stubbed it out?'

Reynolds gazed at him glumly.

'Fazakerly is left-handed,' Gently said. 'And you've got a dab from a right-hand finger.'

He picked up the pin again, weighing it, balancing it. It had plainly not been intended for use on a yacht. It was over a foot long and probably weighed three pounds: more likely it had been salvaged from one of the big barges. But it was lethal . . . oh yes! A tap from that would crack a skull. And however angry you were, when you picked it up, its weight would give you pause unless your intention was to kill . . .

Yes: a killer's weapon. You could rule out manslaughter.

'Are you busy for an hour?'

Reynolds shook his head lyingly. He could scarcely be anything else than busy, but one didn't argue with Gently.

'Let's go over to the flat, then, and you can fill me in on the spot.'

Reynolds bowed his head and opened the door. He didn't even leave a message.

Bland Street, Chelsea, was a short cul-de-sac ending with the block of flats called Carlyle Court. They had been built during the concrete phase of the 'thirties and had the air of a set from *Things To Come.* Slab fronts, in a medley of planes, concluded in small square towers roofed with copper domes, and the porch, a lofty Babylonian concept, carried giant bas-reliefs of wrestling women.

Reynolds rang and they were admitted by an elderly porter in a wine-coloured uniform.

'This is Dobson,' Reynolds said. 'He let Fazakerly in on Monday.'

'What time was that?' Gently asked.

'Half past three, sir,' Dobson said.

'You're sure of the time?'

'Oh yes, sir, definitely. That clock up there had just chimed the half-past.'

He spoke defensively, a faded old man with a waxed walrus moustache, standing peering up at Gently, his dulled eyes puckered and straining.

'You know Fazakerly well, of course.'

'Oh yes, sir. Been here several years.'

'What did you make of him?'

'Cheery, sir. Always had a kind word.'

'Where did he leave his car on Monday?'

'Out front there, like always.'

'Like always?'

'He was never in long, sir. Always out and about, that's Mr Fazakerly.'

'He parked his car, and you admitted him. Did you have any conversation?'

'Well, just a few words, sir. You know how it is. Like if he'd had a good weekend, something like that.' What sort of mood was he in?'

'Cheery, sir. Never known him any different.'

'Why didn't you see him go out again?'

'I must have been doing the boiler, sir.'

Gently nodded. He was conscious of a faint fragrance pervading the thickly-carpeted hall, the walls of which, rising to the height of the second storey, were ornamented with alcoves and thick gilded grilles.

'Who runs this place?'

'Mr Stockbridge, sir. He's the manager, he is.'

'Where can I find him?'

'He'll be in his office, sir. Down this corridor and on the right.'

Gently led the way down the corridor, which had plastered walls with a coloured stipple, and found a slab door painted plum red and lettered: C. F. Stockbridge (Manager). He knocked, and a voice told him to come in. They entered a large room with no windows. Instead, it was lit by concealed lights from behind panels on each of the four walls. A man rose from a desk spread with papers.

'Oh, it's you, Inspector,' he said. 'I was wondering when you'd look in . . . tell me, when shall we get possession?'

He was a dark-haired man in his forties, dressed in an expensive lounge suit. He wore an exquisite silk bow tie and had a red carnation in his button-hole.

'You see, these places aren't chicken-feed, and it's my job to see they're never empty. Frankly, Fazakerly couldn't pay the rent, and you know what claiming on the estate is like . . .'

He gave Gently a sharp glance.

'Do I know this gentleman?' he asked Reynolds.

Reynolds murmured Gently's name.

'Ah!' Stockbridge said. 'More red tape.'

He drew out a slim cigarette-case-cum-lighter and lit a cigarette without offering them round. The room, apart from the desk and a single filing-cabinet, was furnished more like a lounge than an office. Stockbridge sprayed smoke over their heads, eyed Gently again, but said nothing.

'How much is their rent?' Gently asked.

'The Fazakerlys? Two hundred a month. Perhaps you'll understand now—'

'When did they come here?'

'When? Oh, they've been here five years.'

'So you know them well?'

'I wouldn't say that. It's not my place to mix with the tenants. I see them, yes, we have a drink at Christmas. But I don't know anything about their business.'

'You knew which one held the purse-strings.'

'Well, that was pretty obvious, wasn't it? Mrs Fazakerly wrote all the cheques. It's easy to spot a set-up like that.'

'What sort of set-up, Mr Stockbridge?'

'Where it's the wife who calls the tune. Where the husband is just the boy round the place, a pet poodle in trousers.'

He stared fiercely at Gently. In a flashy way he had good looks; dark eyes, a tanned complexion, white teeth which he showed frequently. Yet there was a spivvishness in his manner, perhaps in the nattiness of his clothes. You might have placed him as a car-salesman or a high-pressure estate agent.

'And Fazakerly accepted this situation?'

'I don't want to run the fellow down. I felt sorry for him, rather. I've got no quarrel with Fazakerly.'

'Did they ever have rows?'

'Not in public, anyway. In fact, you rarely saw them out together. Fazakerly has his interests, sailing, photography. I doubt if he was in the flat very much.'

'Had he other women?'

Stockbridge shrugged. 'Better ask him. He wouldn't have a damn sight to run them on. And he wouldn't and didn't bring them here. Be no point in that, would there?'

'There might have been someone here already.'

'Possible. We don't check on tenants' morals.'

'A neighbour.'

'Could be.'

'Say, Mrs Bannister?'

Stockbridge stared at him, shook his head.

'But she was a friend of theirs, wasn't she?'

'Not of his. And anyway, you'd better forget that angle. Take it from me there's nothing in it. He was no chum of Sybil Bannister's.'

He didn't take his eyes off Gently.

'I'm telling you what you know, aren't I?' he said. 'I daresay it's pretty notorious, but it's inside the law. We couldn't clamp down on them.'

'They made it fairly obvious, did they?'

'Let's say you didn't have to wonder too much.'

'And Fazakerly accepted that too?'

'Apparently. I don't know what was going on.'

He took a few quick draws at his cigarette, then

turned to stub it out in a big silver ashtray. Though he was probably being quite frank he still gave a curious impression of insincerity.

'Who were their other friends?' Gently asked.

'I'm afraid I can't help you there. She has a sister of course, I don't know her name. Fazakerly would have his sailing pals.'

'Where were you when it happened?'

'Me? I was in the City. On the first Monday of each month I show my accounts at head office.'

'Where's that?'

'In Old Broad Street. The Associated Holdings and Development Co.'

'You didn't see Fazakerly that day?'

'I haven't seen him since Friday.'

Gently had no more questions. Stockbridge followed them to the doorway. His last gambit, like his first, was:

'But when are we going to get possession . . . ?'

They took a silent, gentle, plush-lined lift from the hall to the seventh floor, issuing out on a broad landing lit by a rooflight of thick green glass. The landing was treated as an anteroom and had green wall-to-wall carpeting, three chairs, formed from bended green glass, and a small table of like material. The walls were finished in green plaster with a pattern of whorls. There were two doors, also green, but the smaller of them probably served a closet.

'Who are the neighbours?' Gently asked.

'There aren't any, Chief . . . not up here. There's a

penthouse flat on the other side of the block, but of course that doesn't connect with this.'

'Who's underneath?'

'Mrs Bannister.'

'Does she go in for this sort of décor?'

Reynolds apparently thought this a joke, for he gave a conscious sort of snigger.

He unlocked the larger of the doors. They went through into a long hallway. It too was lit by green glass rooflights and had the same submarine character as the landing. On the walls, in moulded glass frames, hung a series of Japanese prints of fish; fat, voluptuous, swirling monsters with sad eyes and gaping mouths. Glass furniture was ranged beneath them and at the end of the hall stood a glass fountain. It was in the form of a nymph who poured water from a glass pitcher into a glass rock-pool.

'That was working . . . I switched it off. There's a tank of green-coloured water. Everything's the same except in Fazakerly's room. She was a blonde, maybe that explains it.

'She was more than a blonde,' Gently grunted.

'You should see the bathroom. And her bedroom.'

'Just now, I'd sooner see the lounge.'

'It's this door on the right.'

The lounge was a handsome room with a long veranda which looked over roofs to the Albert Bridge. From any one of its ten windows you could see a stretch of the river. It was furnished expensively, not in glass, but with neo-Victorian stuffed furniture. Curtains of heavy apple-green velvet swathed windows and door. The carpet was a green Persian and there were green Chinese vases in an alcove, and supporting the alcove, in green carved frames, two Etty, or near-Etty, nudes. A book-case painted in the prevailing colour contained books bound in a soapy green calf; they were poets of a romantic cast mingled with some Oriental erotica. On a low tray-table stood six jade figurines of posturing female nudes, while a green soapstone sculpture, on a japanned base, frankly symbolized a female genital organ. A bronze incense-burner stood near it. A perfume of cypress pervaded the room.

'Where was the belaying-pin kept?'

Reynolds pointed to a section of varnished pin-rail. It was fastened to the wall between two of the windows and partly hidden by the fall of the curtains. In effect it was exactly behind the vast settee on which Mrs Fazakerly's body had been discovered. If she were sitting on the settee one could have seized the pin and struck her all in one movement.

'Not very obvious, Chief . . . up there?'

No: not very obvious at all. In fact, if the curtains had been allowed to fall naturally, it would have been hidden altogether. Meanwhile, distributed about the room, were several alternative weapons: the incense-burner, the bit of soapstone, two silver candle-sticks, a green glass door-stop.

'Fazakerly would know where to go for it. A stranger here wouldn't know.'

'But why?' Gently grunted. 'Why go for a weapon that had his name on it?'

'I'd say it was the natural weapon for him. He was crazy mad and he went straight for it.'

'If he was crazy mad he wouldn't go round there. He'd grab that bronze job or a candlestick. Was there blood on the floor?'

'Well . . . some splashes.'

'But she was killed on the settee, where the mess is?'

Reynolds nodded.

'So at the height of this row she was calmly sitting there, watching Fazakerly go after the pin.'

'We don't know exactly . . .'

'But does it make sense?'

Reynolds shrugged his shoulders diplomatically.

'It doesn't,' Gently snorted. 'It's a different picture. It's a picture of something much more calculated.'

He went behind the sofa.

'This makes more sense. She's sitting there quietly talking to someone. Someone who knows what they're going to do and what the weapon's going to be. Someone who's moved across to the window, who's saying something about the view, about the curtains . . . then, before she can move to defend herself, out comes the pin and she's had it. Isn't that more convincing?'

'But there was a row, Chief . . .'

'Wait a minute, here's something more! Suppose Fazakerly was mad enough to use that pin, why didn't he then throw her over the veranda?'

'The veranda . . . ?'

'Yes – seven floors up – did she fall or was she pushed? Then a quick mop-up job on the settee, and it's better than evens he'd get away with it.'

Reynolds didn't say anything. He stood looking unhappily at the settee. It suggested, perhaps more than words could, that Gently was beginning to overplay his hand.

'All right . . . forget it for the moment!'

'But . . . surely he'd panic a bit . . . after . . .

'Forget it. I'm just throwing out ideas.'

Nevertheless, Reynolds went to stare over the veranda.

Gently jammed his pipe into his mouth and made a big business of lighting it. Making a firm enemy of Reynolds was about all he'd get out of championing Fazakerly. So there were loose ends and discrepancies – wasn't it always so, on any case? Were you never surprised by illogical details, even in cases where the main facts were indisputable? Much more important than the position of the pin-rail was Fazakerly's awareness that the pin had been used, his being seen running down the stairs, the equivocal impression he made. The last especially would weigh with a jury. It had hung more men than had hard fact.

Reynolds came back in.

'I don't think it was on, Chief.'

'Never mind about that. Just give me a timetable.'

'Somebody would have seen him from the street . . .'

'We're wasting time. Let's get to facts.'

According to medical evidence Clytie Fazakerly had died at between two and four p.m. on the Monday. She was last seen alive, except by Fazakerly, by Mrs Bannister, with whom she had lunch. She left Mrs

Bannister's flat at about two-forty p.m. She was in good spirits; they had planned, in the evening, a visit to a club cabaret in Soho. At three-thirty p.m. Fazakerly returned from his weekend sailing trip. A little later Mrs Bannister heard sounds of an altercation in the flat above. Altercations between the Fazakerlys were not unusual but this one sounded particularly violent and Mrs Bannister came out on her landing the better to hear what was going on. She heard Fazakerly calling his wife names in an angry manner. She also heard Mrs Fazakerly say something like: 'So you'll drop this bitch, or I'll—!' Soon after that the voices stopped and she heard the slamming of a door, then quick footsteps on the stairs, and she saw Fazakerly running down them. His face was pale and his eyes wild-looking. He didn't notice Mrs Bannister. Her indicator told her the lift was in use, which she supposed was why Fazakerly was using the stairs. She was concerned, but not alarmed, and decided not to intrude on Mrs Fazakerly. At four-twenty-five p.m. the body was discovered by the Fazakerlys' housekeeper, a Mrs Lipton, who had a free period on Monday and was not due to arrive until four-thirty p.m. The body was in a sitting position on the settee and the belaying-pin lay on the floor a few feet distant. Mrs Lipton rushed down the stairs and informed Mrs Bannister, who immediately telephoned the police.

'Any signs of a struggle?' Gently grunted.

'No.'

'Had she tried to defend herself?'

'Apparently not.'

'She'd just been sitting there, suspecting nothing, in the middle of a violent row with her husband?'

Reynolds was beginning to turn red. 'We don't know she was sitting there. She may have been standing up, perhaps she'd turned her back on him. Then he could have caught her and sat her on the settee. He could have stunned her first. We can't rule it out.

'In that case he must have picked up the belaying-pin earlier, which you can hardly suppose she didn't notice.'

'He may have concealed it . . .'

'You try concealing it!'

Well, I don't know . . . I'm damned sure he did it.'

'Listen,' Gently said. 'The voices stop, the door slams and Fazakerly's running. At the most he'd only have time to dot her once: anything else would be impossible. And then she'd have fallen with a thump, and Mrs Bannister heard no thump. What she's describing isn't murder, it's the conclusion of a row.'

'But with everything else . . .'

'Who was using the lift?'

Reynolds stared uncomprehendingly. 'He ran down the stairs—'

'Because the lift was in use! But who was using the lift just then?'

'Well, one of the tenants—'

'Have you checked?'

Reynolds slowly shook his head.

'If we lay off Fazakerly for a moment,' Gently said, 'perhaps we can start seeing some other things straight.

For instance, there's half an hour between when Fazakerly left and when Mrs Lipton discovered the body. Plenty of time for another visitor – and the lift was in use as he was leaving.'

'But there's nobody else in the picture.'

'Has she left a will?'

Reynolds nodded.

'So?'

'She's left a few hundred to the housekeeper, but the bulk of it goes to the woman downstairs.'

'How much?'

'Nearly two hundred thousand.'

'And Fazakerly gets nothing?'

'Not a sou. But just a moment! Mrs Bannister is rolling in it. She's the widow of Fletcher Bannister, the plastics magnate.'

'All the same, it puts her in the picture, and you'll have to admit she had opportunity.'

'It won't wash, Chief, really it won't. You'd do better to blame the job on a burglar.'

No, it wouldn't wash. None of this by-play was going to wash. It had the ingenuity of a desperate defence which would sound so persuasive in a printed record. But recite the facts, put Fazakerly in the box, and no bunch of red herrings would get him off. It didn't need Reynolds to tell Gently that his finesses were convincing neither of them.

'All right,' he sighed. 'Let's look at the bathroom.'

Reynolds ushered him to it with an air of relief. It was comparatively small, but had been entirely modelled to resemble a grotto of green crystal. It had no window. At the pressure of a switch it was suffused by a dim, subterranean glow, and water was fed to the bath, which was sunken, from inlets concealed beneath the rim. Three extended fingers of a glass hand were levers operating the supply.

'Would you credit it?' Reynolds marvelled. 'Where do they sell this sort of thing, anyway?'

He reached out and moved one of the fingers.

'Ugh!' he said. 'It's bloody obscene!'

They went next door into the bedroom, which appeared completely dark as they entered it, but after a moment one saw that the windows, two large ones, still filtered light through bottle-green glass cubes.

'Where's the switch?'

'Wait a moment . . . this is it.'

Reynolds fumbled around and located a silk bell-pull. But the light he produced was so feeble and diffused that it scarcely improved what came from the windows. At last one could see a huge four-poster bed, almost as wide as it was long, a low divan, or padded bench, and a big semi-circular stuffed chair. The floor was completely carpeted over what felt like a deep foam base and the walls and ceiling were thickly quilted in green silk with jade studs. The door was similarly quilted. When it closed it seemed to vanish. The air in the room, though apparently fresh, was warm and charged with the odour of cypress.

'Look over here, Chief!'

Reynolds had lowered his voice, and was pointing furtively to a wall bracket. Hanging from it was a small whip with a bush of very fine thongs. Gently took it down. It had a silver handle set with what may have been emeralds. The thongs were silk and carried no weight. You could barely have swatted a fly with it. He put it back.

'Just a toy.'

'Yes . . . she didn't intend to get hurt, did she? Then there are these.'

He showed some plaited silk cords which had been lying over the back of the chair.

'Did she actually sleep in this room?'

'Yes. That's what I asked Fazakerly.'

'Quite a woman.'

'She was queer as hell, Chief. If you ask me, she had it coming to her.'

They went out again into the corridor, the door closing noiselessly behind them. Reynolds, eager to show all the gimmicks, switched on the fountain and stood admiring it. As he had said, the water was green. It fell with a tinkle in the glass basin.

'Well . . . that's about it, Chief. What do you really think . . . now?'

'I think he's guilty,' Gently said.

'He is. You don't have to worry about that.'

'Just the same.'

Reynolds nodded. 'I'll see it's tied up a bit tighter. This'll do me some good, this case, I'm not going to slip up on the details. Can I charge him now?'

Gently made a face. 'Let it stick till tomorrow lunchtime. That'll give me an alibi with the family.'

'As you like, Chief. It's all one to me.'

They took a cursory glance at the rest of the flat,

including Fazakerly's untidy bedroom; then, on the landing, Gently pointed to the second door.

'What do they keep in that?' he asked.

'It's just a boxroom.'

Reynolds shoved open the door. Inside was a stack of expensive luggage. Colourful labels, now marked and rubbed, spoke of Paris, Cannes, Monaco, Capri.

'Did you find the door locked when you came here?'

Reynolds frowned, said: 'I don't remember.'

'That's fresh cigarette ash down there.'

'That'd probably be Buttifant. He always has a fag on.'

Gently nodded, remembering Buttifant, a sad-faced man who smoked self-rolled cigarettes.

Just his trademark on the floor.

What was the point of trying too hard?

CHAPTER THREE

IN THAT CASE, why was he still hesitating, while the two of them stood waiting for the lift to ascend? Not because of his celebrated intuition: that was backing Reynolds all the way! Nor was it for any family reason. Honour was satisfied there. Already he was choosing the words he would use to Geoffrey ('I checked each stage of the case . . . frankly, it was hopeless.') So what was it?

He turned to Reynolds. 'I think I'll talk to the Bannister woman, since I'm round here.'

Reynolds looked at him quickly. 'You're still not satisfied—?'

'Oh yes. But I'm bloody curious too.'

And that was the fact of the matter: he was bloody curious too. Not about Fazakerly, who he'd written off, but about that surprising woman, his victim. Clytie Fazakerly, invert, voluptuary, who had whored her way to a big fortune, who'd created this strange green mansion, and along with it the germ of her own destruction. A laudable motive? Perhaps not! But a strong motive, without doubt. And who could say that it might not lead him to . . . well . . . some truth, some new understanding. In his profession, at his rank, a degree of creative latitude was defensible . . .

'If you don't mind, Chief, I'll get along. I'm expecting Buttifant from Rochester.'

'Good. Let me know if you find any bloodstains.'

'Of course, Chief. I'll keep in touch.'

The lift arrived, but on second thoughts Gently went down by the stairs: those same stairs which Fazakerly had run down, at the same hour, three days previously. They were prosaic enough. They proceeded in a single flight to the floor below, bare concrete treads with a steel handrail and lit by a clumsy, industrial-pattern wall lamp-unit. Glass panelled swing doors gave access to them from the end of each landing. From the foot of one flight you passed the doors to the top of the next flight down.

Gently came to the sixth-floor landing. It was more impersonal than the one above. A varnished sign-board pointed to a hallway and was lettered: FLATS 21–25. The landing however was similarly carpeted and had its own quota of chairs, while in place of the boxroom on the other landing was an illuminated basin in which goldfish swam.

He rang the bell of Flat 20. The door was answered by a maid. She wore a neat uniform and apron and make-up which carried pinkness above the cheekbones.

'Please?'

Her accent was un-English.

'Chief Superintendent Gently. I'd like to speak to Mrs Bannister.'

'Oh, yes, thank you. Please wait here.'

Behind her she left a fulsome fragrance which suggested poppies or chrysanthemums. Gently heard her tap at an inner door and say something unintelligible in her lisping twitter. 'Who?' a powerful voice demanded. 'Very well. Show him in, Albertine.' Albertine re-appeared and made a slight curtsey.

'Please, Monsieur is to enter.'

He was shown into a room corresponding to the lounge in the flat above, but there was no nonsense about this room, though it was expensively furnished. On the floor lay an Indian carpet which may have cost four figures, and three Kashmir rugs which would have totalled little less. A settee and set of six chairs and a bow-fronted cabinet were Sheraton, and there was a Chippendale bureau-bookcase faced by a Chinese Chippendale chair. Some other good pieces had been quietly added. There was glass and lustre in the cabinet. A single large picture, apparently a Wilson, occupied the end wall above a Sheraton side-table. But in all, though these furnishings would have set a connoisseur's eye roving, the general impact of the room was of expensive restraint.

'You have come about poor Clytemnestra again?'

A woman had risen from the settee to meet him. She was tall, in her forties, and had straight black hair, and the hair was parted in the centre and drawn into brackets round her face. She wore a severe green dress with a square neck and no sleeves. She was appraising Gently with intense, chocolate-brown eyes.

'Mrs Bannister?'

'Yes. But I don't think I know you, do I?'

Gently shook his head. I'm from the Central Office. I'm merely advising on the case.'

'The Central Office! Isn't that the Yard?'

'Until they build us new premises.'

'But I thought—'

'We sometimes confer with our colleagues on a case.'

Her brown eyes regarded him challengingly. She had intelligent, patrician features; a straight nose, rather lank cheeks, and a firm, though delicately-rounded, chin. She used no make-up. On her dress was pinned a large silver brooch set with an agate.

'Of course, I know nothing of these affairs, and I should prefer to retain my ignorance, but isn't it unusual for you to be consulted on such a straightforward case?'

Gently shrugged. 'Is it straightforward?'

'I don't see how you can make it a mystery. It isn't a mystery to me, I assure you, and I made a plain statement of what I know of it. Have you caught him yet?'

'He came to my office.'

'Ah, that explains it – trust Siggy to be devious!'

'Siggy?'

'His second name is Sigismund. For some reason, Siggy seemed to suit him.'

'I take it you didn't like him, Mrs Bannister.'

She made a beautifully controlled gesture. 'In the end I didn't care either way, because I saw very little of him. He was about as conspicuous as an outdoor cat and had much the same place in Clytemnestra's household. She fed him and gave him a corner on a wet night. That was all.'

'They were completely estranged.'

'If you wish.'

'She didn't care what he did with himself.'

'Oh dear! Do you need me to make it plainer? If he'd done it quietly, he might have gone and hung himself.'

'That's been my impression,' Gently said.

'I'm glad, so glad. I thought you had missed it.'

'But doesn't that make it a little strange that they should quarrel violently over another woman?'

Her bold eyes challenged him again, implying an impertinence to be stared down.

'Well,' she said, 'you'd best take a seat. If you want to be clever, it will take time.'

Gently silently chose a Sheraton chair and turned it back to the windows. Mrs Bannister frowned at him for some seconds, then went to give a tug to a tasselled bell-pull. Albertine entered. Mrs Bannister addressed her in a stream of resonant French. Albertine curtseyed and withdrew. Mrs Bannister took her seat on the settee. She caught Gently's eye.

'Well?'

'I was wondering . . . is your maid's name really Albertine?'

'It most certainly is. There would be no satisfaction in having a false Albertine.' Her stare held for a moment, then she grudgingly gave him a smile. 'For a policeman,' she said, 'you seem to be a very determined reader.'

'Did you get her by accident?'

'Oh no. One must take trouble over worthwhile things. We interviewed maids by the dozen in Paris before we discovered *our* Albertine.'

'We?'

'Does that surprise you? Clytemnestra was no illiterate. And here's a little test for you, Superintendent: Albertine actually comes from Illiers.'

Gently shook his head. 'I'd have to look that up . . .'

'Then I'll save you the trouble. Illiers is Combray.'

Now her smile was triumphant, but it quickly faded again.

'And all that's past,' she said dully. 'As though it had never been . . . so suddenly. And what should be Wagner splitting the skies is just Cole Porter in the next room.'

'Yet you're wearing no mourning.'

She pointed to her dress. 'Not mourning as you'd understand it. But this is the colour she'd expect, the colour of death and love. Her colour: she was the Green Lady. That was the myth she made real.'

'The myth . . . ?'

Mrs Bannister nodded. 'Of the woman untouchable by man. The perfect species, the type of the race, from which the male is a biological splinter. You are aware I suppose, being so well read, that that is the current scientific view?'

Gently hunched. 'Biology isn't my subject.'

'Then you may accept the fact from me. The male is a departure from the norm, a specialized carrier of the seed. Probably as a reaction to his situation, which is one of biological inferiority, he has developed an aggressive and self-glorifying ego which in turn has given rise to an unstable society. The biological direction is plain and evident. It is towards a diminished status of the male.'

'You mean matriarchy?'

'More than that. The role of the male is biologically narrow. He carries the seed and transmits it. That is his solitary function.'

'Perhaps, but you'll hardly do without it . . .'

'You have heard of artificial insemination?'

'Yes, but there are psychological factors—'

'Not for me. Not for Clytemnestra.'

She rested her chin on her clasped hands and stared large-eyed from between her brackets. She was sitting on the settee with her legs tucked under her and had a curious pixie-like appearance. Though she was tall she was perfectly made. She had a firm, unconscious femininity.

'Of course, you'll have talked to Siggy about us, and no doubt he gave us some pretty names. You'd rather expect that, wouldn't you? The poor creature was living out of his century. But you've come to me now – correct me if I'm wrong – to hear the other side of the picture, and I'm perfectly willing to give it to you. You seem a man of intelligence.'

'Thank you. There were other questions—'

'Oh, let's put our cards on the table! I'm an invert, and so was she, and we were neither proud nor ashamed of it. Quite simply, we are the New Women.'

'New . . . ?'

'Speaking biologically. We are the vanward of the trend towards a more successful racial pattern. In this the males will decline, probably in numbers as well as status, and with them will decline the factor of social instability. This is a perfectly logical trend, following the law of natural selection. By means of diminished heterosexuality, the race proceeds to greater stability. And in that sense you must term women like us the New Women.'

'And male inverts the New Men?'

'Why not? They are part of the same pattern. They are diminishing heterosexuality, and so assisting the trend.'

'So that, eventually, in a society which is predominantly female, heterosexuality will be an inversion, and present inversion the norm?'

She shook her head. 'Don't you see that then there can be no inversion – that heterosexuality will become simply the transmission of seed? On the one hand you will have love, a physico-spiritual expression, and on the other insemination. There is nothing left to call inversion.'

'Is there anything left to call love?'

'Now you're beginning to slip a century.'

Gently's shoulders twitched. 'What's a century,' he asked, 'to the law of natural selection? Did Mrs Fazakerly hold this theory?'

'Yes. If you can think of no better term.'

'And it involved her in whips and cords?'

'My God,' she said. 'You sound like Siggy.'

★ ★ ★

There was a tap at the door and Albertine entered with a tea-tray. It was a Georgian tray with a shell-pattern border and carried a silver tea-service of the same period. Mrs Bannister rose and fetched a small table and placed it by the settee. Albertine set the tea-tray on the table. Mrs Bannister dismissed her in French.

'Was she here on Monday?' Gently asked.

'No. We give the servants Monday off.'

'You were alone?'

'I was alone. Do you take milk, Superintendent?'

She handed Gently his tea. It was in a fluted cup which doubtless bore a mark of crossed swords, along with a silver spoon with a rat-tailed bowl and trellis-engraving on the shank. The tea was slightly aromatic. Mrs Bannister drank it with a squeeze of lemon. While she drank she watched Gently, her large eyes tight with aggression. Finally she took a cigarette from a vanity bag lying on the settee and lit it with a tiny wax match, and breathed smoke once or twice.

'No doubt I over-estimate you,' she said. 'After all, you're still a policeman. You'll have the moral attitudes of a policeman. You wouldn't dare not to have, would you? For you, sex is fundamentally distasteful, and you wish the Almighty had ordered it otherwise. But since he hasn't, then it's your duty to keep the lid on the sewer. Your point of view is a little blasphemous, but the Almighty must shoulder some blame for that.'

She flicked her cigarette waspishly.

'May I smoke my pipe?' Gently asked.

'Please do. I shall have the room squished after you've gone in any case.'

'What did you talk about at lunch on Monday?'

'Is it any of your business?'

'You told my colleague the deceased was in good spirits. Yet she was quarrelling bitterly a short time afterwards.'

Mrs Bannister closed her eyes. 'Couldn't you have used some other word?' she said. 'Deceased: just a word in a report. It's so pitifully inadequate.'

'Did she mention her husband and this woman?'

'She didn't mention her husband at all. He wasn't a topic of conversation. We were discussing autumn fashions.'

'Nothing else?'

'Our evening arrangements.'

'Her husband's affair wasn't even hinted at?'

'Not even a hint. I can tell you quite certainly that nothing was further from her mind. She burst in, as she always did, full of fun and high spirits. She brought some sketches from Waring with her, I daresay you'll find them upstairs. We had them spread all over the floor. She was very excited about the new line. During lunch we were choosing a coat for her and deciding about accessories. Then we discussed what to wear that evening, but she soon returned to the sketches, and she went out planning to ring for an appointment. That was what her mind was full of.'

'But she'd have mentioned this woman on a previous occasion.'

'Perhaps it would help if I knew who she was.'

'Don't you know?'

'I'm afraid not. I've never been much interested in Siggy's women.'

'But you knew he had them, and so did Mrs Fazakerly.'

Mrs Bannister breathed smoke delicately. 'I have to give you the point,' she said. 'I find that quarrel of theirs incomprehensible. Nobody cared about Siggy's women. He was always sleeping about somewhere. If anything, I imagine Clytemnestra encouraged it, it provided an emotional sedative for him. She knew about some of them, because she used to joke about them, and I'm willing to swear that's all it meant to her.'

'Yet you heard the quarrel.'

'Only a word or two.'

'Enough.'

Mrs Bannister nodded. 'She was being hysterical, and about a woman. She was warning Siggy to drop her, or she'd stop his money. I suppose he confirms it?'

'Oh yes.'

'Who was the woman?'

'A Sarah Johnson.'

'Clytemnestra never mentioned her to me. I'm afraid I'm mystified by the whole business.'

She stared thoughtfully at Gently, as though holding him to blame for her mystification. Perhaps she would liked to have denied the truth of anything about Clytie Fazakerly to which she was not privy. She had drawn her legs in beneath her again and sat curiously upright, without support.

'Had Mrs Fazakerly any relatives?'

'Only her step-father and the Merryn woman. Her step-father is a solicitor in Bristol and he'd ceased to have anything to do with her. Brenda Merryn is her half-sister, a doctor's receptionist or some such person. I've seen her here a few times. She meant nothing to Clytemnestra.'

'Had she any close friends?'

Mrs Bannister eyed him, but contented herself with a 'No'.

'Well, acquaintances who might visit her?'

'We invited few people here.'

'But you can name one or two?'

'Oh, our friends are mostly about town. People you meet going around. You'd really waste your time investigating them. Anyway, where's the point, Superintendent? The facts of the case are not in dispute. Siggy killed her. I know it. You know it. It was on his face when I saw him.'

Gently nodded. 'When you saw him, you say the lift was in use?'

'Yes. The numbers were flashing. I don't know why I particularly noticed it.'

'Was the lift coming up or going down?'

'I don't remember. Wait! – coming up.'

'You're certain?'

'Yes . . . I can see the numbers.'

'And would you remember where it stopped?'

She looked away, then quickly back at him. 'Now we're being clever again,' she said. 'No, I don't know where it stopped, but I can tell you certainly where it didn't. It didn't stop on these two floors. If it had stopped on this one I would have seen it. If it had gone past I would have heard it. Ergo, it stopped lower down.'

'Did you hear or see it later on?'

'No, because I was not in the hall.'

'So it, or the stairs, might well have been used, and you would not have been the wiser.'

She breathed smoke silently for some moments, giving it little, modulated utterances, then she said:

'You know, I don't think I understand you, Superintendent. Have you some reason for supposing that Siggy didn't do it?'

'He says he didn't.'

She shrugged contemptuously. 'What was he likely to say? And don't forget he's an arrant liar, though you may have discovered that for yourself.'

Gently nodded. 'There are also some other points.'

'What are they?'

'Points of detail. For instance, what had he to gain by killing her, when she was leaving her money to you?'

Mrs Bannister gave a short laugh. 'So you know about that, do you?' she said. 'Oh, the minds of these policemen! And of course, I'm immediately under suspicion.'

'I didn't say that—'

She raised her hand. 'Please! We can manage without hypocrisy. I don't mind you suspecting me, it gives me a bitter sort of amusement. I am worth suspecting, oh yes, I am perfectly cast for the murderer. Nobody was better situated than myself to have gone up there and killed Clytemnestra. I heard the quarrel, I saw him run off, I could easily have gone in to console her. And then, remembering the money she was going to leave me, I could have reached that belaying-pin down from the wall. I'd know where to go for it, you see, because it was hung there at my suggestion.'

Gently stared at her over his pipe. 'Yes,' he said. 'That fits exactly.'

'Doesn't it? Exactly? And I'm an invert into the bargain.'

She was breathing a little fiercely, and she stubbed out her cigarette with venom. She had large though well-proportioned hands and the fingers looked strong.

'Then all I had to do was wait for Lipton, phone the police and get in my story. And the longer it took them to find Siggy, the more convinced they'd be of his guilt. Well, Superintendent, if I were you I think I'd arrest me on the spot. Or did I leave something out – something that raises a minor doubt?'

Gently stared, didn't say anything. She got up quickly from the settee.

'Now I'll just show you something,' she said. 'Something that's bound to raise your interest.'

She strode across to the bureau-bookcase and unlocked one of the drawers. From it she took two folded documents, each secured with red tape. She exhibited them to Gently so that he could read the titles. They were the wills of Clytemnestra Anne Fazakerly and Sybil Edith Elizabeth Bannister.

'Didn't I say you'd be interested?' she jeered. 'These are the veritable documents. We made them together four years ago, leaving our money to each other. There, please examine the signatures – I want you to be certain these are not copies.'

They were not copies. She flipped over the sheets to show him the signatures and seals, watching, her eyes intent, for any change in his expression.

'There,' she said, 'the disposal of above half a million pounds is in these documents. What do you make as a Chief Superintendent? Vaguely four figures? Something like that?'

Gently shrugged woodenly. 'I make what I earn,' he said.

'Oh, I see – and I earn nothing – on every count I'm despicable!'

'Do you earn something?'

'No. Not a penny. I've lived on society all my life. So you can despise me from the height of your righteousness – I am a criminal before I start.'

'Why are you showing me these wills?'

'Because I'm about to be melodramatic. And that's another ugliness of the social parasite – it insists on dramatizing itself.'

She went to the bell-pull and pulled it. Albertine appeared directly. Mrs Bannister spat some French at her, and she retired hastily and without a curtsey. When she returned she was carrying a chafing-dish, which she placed on a stand before Mrs Bannister. Mrs Bannister dismissed her with a gesture. Then she began opening and crumpling the two wills.

'Am I committing an offence?' she asked.

'A technical offence.' Gently made no motion.

'And you're not going to stop me? How kind! No doubt all is grist to your mill.'

She considered the pile of crumpled paper.

'I think this deserves a libation,' she said. 'Poor Clytemnestra would have enjoyed that touch, also the paper doesn't seem very combustible.'

She went to a tantalus on the side-table and fetched a decanter of cognac. She lifted the decanter high above the dish and let cognac pour from it in a stream. Then she ignited it. A clear, liquid flame spread about the dish and paper, becoming yellow and smoky as the paper began to char. At last the paper burned fiercely, sending angry tongues towards the ceiling.

'There,' Mrs Bannister said, 'Clytemnestra's manes receive again Clytemnestra's gift, and the money can go where it likes. I'll see that Lipton isn't a loser.'

'Does this prove something?' Gently asked.

'If it doesn't, I've wasted a lot of cognac. Just see the hunger in those flames – how they lick from sheet to sheet.'

'If Fazakerly gets off he'll have the money.'

'Never. The deed was in his face.'

'You may not convince a jury of that.'

'Does it matter? With the facts?'

She was staring at the flames in a sort of abstractedness, and now she stiffened and raised her arms. Her fine-featured face, looking downwards, caught a flickering ruddiness from the blaze.

'At least, Fazakerly showed some grief.'

'Crocodile tears. He'd know how to use them.'

'But you'd have no need for crocodile tears. Tears from you would be genuine.'

Her eyes flashed at him across the flames.

'What do you know of grief?' she snapped. 'Some

maudlin hypocrisy in a witness-box would be the extent of your comprehension. Did I offer to exhibit my grief to you?'

Gently shook his head. 'Does one exhibit grief . . . ?'

'Oh, I could exhibit it if I wanted to, if I wasn't too numbed to put on a show!' She let her arms fall. 'But of course,' she said, 'I was forgetting I was suspect too. So sorry. I should have squeezed out a few tears. This would have been such an appropriate moment.'

The flames burned low in the chafing-dish, became searching blue glow-worms, went out. A few browned scraps of paper remained unconsumed in the rustling ash.

'Get out of here,' Mrs Bannister said.

She turned her back on the dish and Gently.

Gently took his leave. He surprised Albertine, who had her ear to the door.

CHAPTER FOUR

THE DIVISIONAL H.Q. was newly-built in a style of sixth-decade New Town, and inside had an air of hearty brightness and aggressive anti-traditionalism. The C.I.D. was on the first floor. It was reached by a sweep of riser-less steps. Flanking the foot of the steps, in strip-work holders, were two potted rubber-plants with dusty leaves. The steps projected from raw brickwork which extended from the hall to the first-floor ceiling, but which was met at the level of the landing by a plastered wall painted dark blue. Reynolds' office was at the end of the landing. It was shaped like a shoe-box and had one end of glass.

Gently went in without knocking. He found Reynolds in conference with Buttifant. They were seated on opposite sides of a formica-topped table on which lay a pair of shoes and some pieces of clothing. Buttifant was peering at these with a magnifier, but Reynolds was smoking and staring out of the window. He threw a sharp glance as the door opened, then ducked his head and rose.

'Well,' Gently said, 'are we any forwarder?'

'We're filling in the story, Chief,' Reynolds said. 'Seems there's no doubt about Fazakerly's sea-trip, though nobody knows why he wasn't drowned.'

'He probably lacks a drowning mark,' Gently said. 'He has a different sort of complexion. Have we found his yacht?'

'At Harwich, where he said. And the owners at Rochester recognized his photograph.'

Gently pointed to the clothing. 'What about those?'

'We're sending them down to the lab now.'

'But there are no obvious stains?'

Reynolds shrugged. 'I did mention her turban hair-style, Chief.'

Gently stared at him, grunting. 'Did her hair-style cushion the blow?' he asked.

'No, but . . .'

'It wouldn't have stopped the blood spurting either – there'd be blood on those clothes, if he struck the blow. I suppose you did find spattered blood?'

'Well, yes . . . on her dress, on the settee . . .'

'Her turban hair-style didn't stop that.'

'In the lab, perhaps.'

'I wouldn't bank on that.'

Buttifant looked up to say: 'I think you're right sir. There's no sign of blood on any of these . . .'

Then he caught a look from Reynolds and took cover again behind his magnifier.

'So, if no blood,' Gently said, 'we'll need to skate lightly around that one. We'd best advise ignoring it altogether and letting defence counsel make the running. Then it'll sound less important, more like a defensive finesse. It's a pity though . . . the prosecutor's office won't be so happy without its blood.'

'But it's not conclusive, Chief—!' Reynolds burst out.

'Oh no,' Gently said. 'Just one of those things. Provided we don't come up with too many, the prosecutor's office will soldier along with them.'

He ignored Reynolds' goaded look and went over to the C.I.D. man's desk, where he could see a manilla folder of prints with *Fazakerly Case* scribbled across it. He turned them over. The divisional men had done a comprehensive job. The sprawled, nod-headed corpse of Clytie Fazakerly had been photographed from a score of angles. Not more than a yard from her slippered feet lay the gleaming belaying-pin, and dark stains covered the shoulders of the dress and peppered the settee-back adjacent. He turned to Reynolds, who had joined him at the desk.

'Let's face it: she was killed where she sat on the settee. Those scatter-marks prove it to the hilt: when she was struck she was precisely there.'

'That doesn't mean Fazakerly couldn't have done it.'

'It means another hole in the ice. I suppose there's nothing in the P.M. report to suggest she was knocked out before she was killed?'

Reynolds shook his head bleakly. 'Just that one depressed fracture.'

'No broken nails?'

'Nothing of that sort. She was hit once, we think from behind.'

'Well, it could have happened. In the middle of a row she may have sat down on the settee, and she may have ignored Fazakerly going behind her and getting the pin down off the wall. Did the housekeeper handle the pin, by the way?'

'Says she didn't,' Reynolds mumbled.

'We'll suggest the pile of the carpet smeared the prints, and that he changed his grip before throwing it down. Those are the tricky points about the actual commission. We're lucky to have a good witness in Mrs Bannister.'

He sorted over some more prints. The last was a portrait which Reynolds had collected. It showed Clytie Fazakerly at full length and wearing nothing but swathes of gauze. She had a curiously round face with large cheek-bones and a squat nose, eyes that seemed to encroach on her forehead, and a chin vanishing beneath pouting lips. A bold, exposed face, resembling the type portrayed in Minoan paintings, having that same quality of belonging to a remote, dawn culture. Her blonde hair was twisted in a turban which accentuated the impression. She had a strong, buoyant body which carried a hint of athleticism.

'Have you contacted her family?' Gently asked.

'They want nothing to do with it,' Reynolds shrugged. 'Her step-father is a solicitor in Bristol. He soon let me know what he thought about her. Then there's her half-sister living in Kensington, she just wanted her name kept out of the papers. You'd think they'd care about the money, but apparently she smelled too high even for that.'

'Did Fazakerly know where the money was going?'

'No. We've got him on that at least. He didn't know his wife had made a will, so he must have been thinking he was going to collect.'

Gently smiled frostily. 'So he may.' He told Reynolds of Mrs Bannister's bonfire. The C.I.D. man listened blankly, his eyes rounded at Gently.

'But shouldn't we pinch her for that?' he asked at last.

Gently shrugged. 'It's up to you. If you can afford the time Mrs Bannister can afford the expense.'

'But what was she getting at?'

'That's easy. She seemed to think she was under suspicion.'

'Mrs Bannister . . . ?'

'She had that impression. It may have been something I said to her.'

'But that's ridiculous!' Reynolds said.

'Of course Quite ridiculous. She even went on to admit how she might have gone up there after she saw Fazakerly leave. She'd have gone to condole with his wife, of course, and she'd find her sitting on the settee, and she'd know exactly where the pin was kept because it was she who chose the spot for it.'

'But Chief, you can't—'

Gently shook his head. 'That would be too convenient, wouldn't it?' he said. 'Still, there's a point about it which does interest us.'

'What's that?'

'It fits.'

★ ★ ★

But the impression he carried away from Reynolds' office was of the disturbing face of the dead woman: it was beautiful, but with a beauty of a distant, half-comprehended time. By present standards it was not beautiful, which was why it was disturbing. Yet you knew immediately that in its own age it was radiant and royal. It carried back to a child-like morning, an Olympian youth of culture, pre-Hellenic, beyond the stamp the Greeks had given to female beauty. It set you fumbling for the clues to it, for vague tidings of an infant world, for a glimpse behind the blank veil raised by a thousand incarnations.

He went down and sat for some moments in his car, just letting that face rest in his mind. Before seeing the photograph he'd begun to picture this woman from what he'd picked up from Fazakerly and Mrs Bannister. But the face altered all his ideas. It had suddenly wiped the record clean. In place of the depraved parasite he had been seeing was this . . . what was it? At the moment, a face!

A face that excused what the woman had been? Not quite: but a face that helped one understand it. For example, she was amoral, and not immoral: to her, morality would be just a sound. She used her body to secure a fortune, well. It was merely an exercise of her power. If she had that power, why not use it? Why be put off by a clash of words? Then again, in service of that power, why not create conditions to heighten its enjoyment? To exploit to the full its mystical sensualism, unknown in her philosophy as sin?

No doubt it was the strength of her amorality which

fascinated the intellectual Mrs Bannister, which drew into a focus her slightly guilty inversion and set her defensively theorizing. For Mrs Bannister was synthetically amoral. She felt the sting of opinion. She had an answer waiting for the condemnation which Clytie Fazakerly would barely notice. And so she would worship that utter insouciance and discover there a mythic quality and perhaps feel herself the priestess of the myth: and exult a little when left in possession of it. For the priestess is an inferior until she embodies the goddess herself.

A motive there? Gently mentally shrugged, then reached forward to turn the ignition key. But he must know more of Clytie Fazakerly before he could let the matter alone. Instead of a right turn towards Millbank he made a left turn towards Kensington. He drove to a block of flats in Knightsbridge Place, parked, and climbed two flights of steps.

'Yes – who are you?'

The door of the flat was being kept ajar by a safety-chain, and the blonde woman who answered it was wearing an embroidered dressing-gown and beaded slippers.

'Are you Miss Merryn?'

'Perhaps. Who are you?'

Gently identified himself.

'Oh, I see. I thought you might be the Press. They've been pestering Daddy ever since it happened.'

She peered sternly at Gently through the gap, a manicured hand straying over her dressing-gown. If he'd been hoping for a resemblance to the dead woman he was disappointed by what he saw. Brenda Merryn was no Clytie Fazakerly. She had the commonplace good looks of the city woman. In any street you would meet a hundred of her going facelessly about their business.

'Well, have you arrested Siggy yet, or have you come to tell me he's done your job for you?'

'Our job . . . ?'

'Oh, it wouldn't be a shock. He's not the sort to face his responsibilities.'

Gently shook his head. 'Fazakerly is in custody. He gave himself up to me this morning.'

'You surprise me. So what do you want, then?'

'Just a chat with you. If it's convenient.'

For a moment he could read a curt refusal in her eyes, then she slid back a cuff to reveal a wristwatch, consulted it and sighed.

'All right then, if you have to. But I can't give you very long. Unlike my sister I work for a living, I have a surgery to attend at five-thirty.'

She unchained the door and admitted him. They passed through a vestibule into a lounge. It was pleasantly furnished in contemporary style and had curtains of gay cretonne. A meal was set on a tray on a leaf-table under the window. It consisted of poached egg on toast, crisp-bread, honey, an apple and a small pot of tea.

'You don't mind my eating while we talk? I'd just got this served when you rang.'

She drew up a chair to the table and began pouring herself a cup of tea.

'I'd offer you some, but it's a tiny pot, it's the way you live when you're alone. At least, it's the way I live, not being able to run to French maids. What do we chat about?'

'About your sister.'

Gently also drew up a chair. In spite of himself he was feeling let down by the disparity between this woman and Mrs Fazakerly. She was blonde, but of a darker colouring, she was not so tall or robust; the quality of the face was simply missing: in Brenda Merryn it was tired sophistication. She had rather the gaunt, shadowful features of contemporary magazine trend. Even her manner of speaking was weary, as though arising from a deep fatigue.

'First, you will kindly understand we are speaking of my half-sister. That's as close a relationship as most people would want to admit to.'

'You are a little the elder, naturally.'

'Don't bother to guess. I'm thirty-nine. Clytie was thirty-six in June. She didn't look it, I probably do.'

'You weren't very intimate, I take it.'

'Not very intimate, no. That doesn't mean to say I steamed with righteousness and cut her dead in the street. After all, I was her only relative, not counting Daddy; and he doesn't count. I'd give her the time of day when I saw her, and pay her a visit once in so often.'

'When was the last time you visited her?'

Brenda Merryn paused to chew.

'Recently,' she said. 'One day last week. On the Friday, I imagine.'

'Was her husband there?'

'No, he'd gone. Down to Rochester, to his woman.'

'His woman?'

'You know about her, don't you? Sarah someone. His latest woman.'

Gently nodded. 'But how did you know about her?'

'Oh, there's no mystery about Siggy's women. I had a chat with him last time I was there. The poor fool is really sent by this one.'

'And Mrs Fazakerly would know too?'

Brenda Merryn paused over her tea-cup. 'Yes,' she said, 'I should think it likely. Siggy wouldn't bother to cover much. You must understand there was nothing between them, they hadn't slept together for a century. Clytie was carrying on with La Bannister, and Siggy was free to do what he liked. I don't suppose he actually discussed his amours with her, but there was no point in him being secretive.'

'They wouldn't have quarrelled over such a thing.'

'On the surface, it seems unlikely.'

'Seems?'

'Well . . . Clytie had a bitch of a temper. If she was in the mood she might have picked on it.'

'In other words, if she wanted to hurt her husband, she could have picked on this as an instrument?'

'Yes, that's possible. It'd be like Clytie. But his having a woman would be nothing to do with it.'

'So what would have something to do with it?'

Brenda Merryn slanted a shoulder. I've told you I wasn't intimate with them,' she said. 'You'd better ask elsewhere. You could try La Bannister.'

'You had no hint of it on your last visit?'

'No. It was all talk about fashion.'

'Mrs Fazakerly was her usual self?'

'Oh, quite. Queen Clytie.'

She poured herself a second cup, then buttered some crisp-bread and spread it with honey. She had a little colour on either cheek-bone and she avoided Gently's eye as she ate. The embroidered dressing-gown was parted hospitably, but to this she paid no attention; or it may have been a deliberate gesture to show she was still a force, though thirty-nine. Her tawny hair, neatly arranged, had the brushed sheen of devoted attention.

'You don't think highly of Mrs Bannister.'

Brenda Merryn bit off crisp-bread. 'She made Clytie worse than she was,' she said. 'She's full of clap-trap about Lesbianism.'

'You'd say she influenced Mrs Fazakerly that way.'

'Of course. Not that Clytie wanted pushing. But La Bannister stuffed her head with nonsense and made a fool of her in general. Then she made trouble with Clytie's friends. She wanted Clytie on her own. And Clytie was too besotted with her to raise a finger in protest.'

'Who were these friends?'

Brenda Merryn munched. 'I'm not so certain I remember. This was all several years ago, when Clytie moved in at Carlyle Court.'

'People with money?'

'Oh, I daresay. But that wasn't the first qualification.'

'Lesbian friends?'

'Exactly.'

'And you remember none of them?'

'Why should I?'

She followed the crisp-bread with a sip of tea.

'Please,' she said, 'don't think I'm prudish. I lead a reasonably chequered life, and I'm used to a medical view of things. There's a dormant slant that way in all women and a lot of us give it a try. It has an advantage men rarely think of, namely it doesn't get you into trouble. There are also a few emotional bonuses which go with the shedding inhibitions, a feeling of biological emancipation, of being on a footing with the male. Oh, there's plenty to be said for it. Only with me it doesn't work.'

'So these were not friends of yours.'

'I'm trying to make that plain.'

'There was never, say, trouble, with any of them?'

'No. They just got the push.'

Now she began on the apple, peeling it with deft, practised movements, pausing once to tilt her wrist for a check with the watch. It was a natural-enough action, yet somehow it just missed of being natural, and she chopped the apple in quarters roughly, making the knife ring on the plate.

'Well, perhaps there is one woman I remember.'

Gently watched her, saying nothing.

'Her name was Beryl, Beryl Rogers, she used to be very strong with Clytie. She was in with La Bannister too, they were both thick with Beryl. But it only lasted a short time. She blotted her copybook somehow.'

'Do you know how?'

'It was several years back, and I never did know the details. Ask Siggy or La Bannister. It's just that her name came to mind.'

'Where did she live?'

'I've no idea.'

'What was her job?'

'I don't know that she had one. Honestly, I wouldn't have remembered her now if you hadn't got me thinking with your questions. Does it matter?'

Gently shrugged. 'We'd like a reason for a row the Fazakerlys had. You say it couldn't have been just his playing around with a woman, so naturally I'm looking for something else.'

'It was during this row that Siggy killed her?'

'She was killed at about that time.'

'And it was over the Sarah woman?'

'In substance, yes.'

She shook her head slowly. 'No, it doesn't make sense,' she said. 'Clytie just wouldn't have cared about that, there must have been something else behind it. But I'm beginning to understand why he did it. He was quite infatuated with this woman at Rochester. If Clytie provoked him about her and threatened to ditch him then she was asking for what she got.'

Gently said: 'He didn't know it, but his wife had willed her money away from him.'

Brenda Merryn fumbled a section of apple. 'Of course, you'll have seen the will,' she said.

'It's very much what you might expect. The housekeeper gets a small legacy.'

'And – the rest?'

'To Mrs Bannister. They made their wills in each other's favour.'

The section of apple fell to the plate. 'The bitch!' Brenda Merryn exclaimed. 'The dirty bitch! And not a penny to her own sister – oh my God, can you credit it?'

Gently permitted his brows to rise. 'But you weren't very intimate, were you?' he asked.

'Not very intimate – she's my sister! Oh! I'm glad now what Siggy did to her!'

'It doesn't make so much difference, Miss Merryn.'

'I'll fight that tramp. She shan't have it.'

'Neither of those wills is in existence.'

'What?'

'Mrs Bannister has destroyed them.'

Brenda Merryn stared at him, her eyes narrowed, her mouth drooped at the corners. She snatched a cigarette from a packet on the table.

'Just what are you trying to tell me?' she demanded.

'The will is destroyed,' Gently said. 'Mrs Bannister burned it in my presence. Which means that the money will go to your brother-in-law, unless he's found guilty of killing his wife.'

'*Unless* he's found guilty!'

Gently hunched his shoulders. 'In that case, it will follow the rule of succession.'

'Meaning me?'

'Your father or you.'

'He won't touch it. It'll come to me.'

She snapped a lighter, lit the cigarette, rose and began pacing up and down. She seemed for the present to have forgotten Gently: her eyes were fixed and seeing nothing. The dressing-gown, its skirt swinging, showed belted thighs pressing past each other. As she paced she smoked fiercely, expelling the smoke through her teeth.

'But why did she do it – what's her game?'

'Mrs Bannister . . . ?'

'Of course! Don't tell me she'd throw away money like that without some dirty trick behind it. So what is it?'

Gently said nothing.

'Listen – what was that bitch doing on Monday?'

'She was in her flat.'

'Yes – and I'll tell you something: the maid has every Monday off! Don't you see? She was alone in there. She could have done it as well as Siggy. And they weren't so sweet together, those two, they had their rows like everyone else.'

'And you're suggesting . . . ?'

'She destroyed the will – that was an act put on to impress you. She could see you weren't quite swallowing Siggy, so she had to duck out from under the will. Because Siggy might not have done it, might he? That's why you're still asking questions!'

'You're a perceptive woman, Miss Merryn.'

'Oh, I've got La Bannister taped. And Siggy denies it?'

'He denies it.'

'I suppose he'd have to, the poor fool.'

She leaned her hip against the table and stared scathingly at Gently. Her body moulded in an elegant foundation garment, emerged through the separating dressing-gown.

'Watch La Bannister,' she said. 'She'll put one over you unless you're careful. You're only a man, understand me? She'll know how to kid you along all right. A woman can always kid a man because he's always ready to believe her: there's always a bed just behind her, and saying Yes is the way towards it. Oh, I'm not saying that's what you have in mind, but it's the psychological attitude. The pattern. When you talk to a woman it's always the first step up the stairs. So just watch out, that's my advice, because I'm telling you – she's a bitch.'

She pushed smoke through her teeth.

'La B. was too much for Siggy,' she said. 'Clytie was still sleeping with him when dear Sybil arrived on the scene. She's the one he ought to have bashed, because then he might have patched it up with Clytie. But he's not the sort to work things out. He's just impulsive and weak.'

'Impulsive?'

She nodded. 'There's nothing solid in Siggy.'

'You seem to know him pretty well.'

'Pretty well.' Her mouth twisted.

'In fact . . . ?'

'Nothing. I should think it's obvious the poor fool had to talk to someone. That's why he slept around so much. But I was different. I was always there.'

'And you were his confidant.'

'If you like. I understood him better than anyone. And I wasn't surprised when I heard what happened. For him, I'd say it was the only way out.'

‘I suppose you didn’t see him on Monday, Miss Merryn?’

She hissed smoke down towards him.

‘No,’ she said. ‘Does he say I did?’

Gently shrugged without replying.

She made a gliding movement with her hips. ‘I’m a working girl, Superintendent,’ she said. ‘On Monday I had my two surgeries, facts which you can easily check.’

‘But in the afternoon?’

‘I was here resting. I like my bath in the afternoon. In fact, I was not long out of it when you came knocking at my door.’ She tilted the watch again, and sighed. ‘I’m afraid I must push you out, Superintendent. It’s time to dress and become formidable – that’s my profession as well as yours.’

Gently rose. She held out a hand with its perfect and finely-polished nails. When he ignored it she shrugged faintly and flickered a smile with her eyes.

‘I’m not dangerous,’ she said. ‘Fairly human, but not dangerous. And don’t be so damned impregnable, because it piques a girl in her undies. You weren’t having me on about that will?’

‘No, Miss Merryn.’

‘The name is Brenda. Then I’ll be rich . . . and I like the idea. Though of course, it’s a rotten shame about Siggy.’

CHAPTER FIVE

THERE WAS A phone-box near where Gently had parked, and when he came down he rang the office. This was insurance, because his rank relieved him of the stricter forms of supervision, but on the present occasion he was switched directly to the C.I.D. Assistant Commissioner.

'Ah, Gently. What are you up to?'

Gently propped himself against the parcel-bin. It wasn't worth while even trying to fool this thin-faced man with his big spectacles. He ran an inter-office espionage system which was second to none in Whitehall, and if he didn't this moment know what Gently was up to, he could have the information one minute later. So Gently told him.

'Yes . . . I see. There was a rumour of this going the rounds. But I'm not sure I like it, you sticking your oar in. How close a relative is he . . . a cousin?'

'My brother-in-law's cousin,' Gently said.

'Did you know him?'

'No.'

'So what's the interest?'

'It was me he came to in the first place.'

The A.C. made impatient noises. 'See here, Gently,' he said, 'let's get this straight. I want a perfectly honest answer – do you think he did it, or don't you?'

'I think he did it.'

'Then what's the beef? Why can't the Chelsea lot handle it?'

'Because he'll probably get off,' Gently said. 'And I'd like to make that point before he's charged.'

The Assistant Commissioner paused, and Gently smiled at the roof of the phone-box. He could see quite plainly the great man's face, its eyes narrowed and suspicious. But he'd have to play along with that one: there had been too many failed prosecutions lately. Better give Gently his head for a bit than risk another expensive acquittal . . .

'Gently.'

'Yes?'

'You're not having me on – there's a genuine chance of Fazakerly getting off?'

'I'd say it was a sixty-forty chance.'

'But damn it, he did it – you're sure of that!'

Gently hunched a shoulder. 'I'm pretty certain, and so will the jury be, too. But not certain enough. The detail evidence is all consistent with his innocence. Then there's the character of the deceased, and alternatives with opportunity and motive. No, unless Fazakerly confesses I can't see us winning this one.'

'Would he confess?'

'Most unlikely.'

'Have you talked to him since this morning?'

'No. But he was decided enough then. And he's a long way from being stupid.'

Another pause. By now the A.C. would have swivelled his chair a little, would be resting his elbow on the desk and throwing a dirty look at the window. He had played much mental chess with Gently. These days he studied the board with care.

'I think you'd better talk to him again, Gently.'

'Yes, I've one or two things to ask him.'

'I daresay you have. But what I'm suggesting is putting pressure on him for a confession.'

'I'm not the man to do that—'

'Oh yes you are, Gently, no one more so. He obviously trusts you or he wouldn't have come to you, so he'll perhaps respond to your advice.'

'But that's doing the dirty—!'

'He's guilty isn't he?'

'He'll get the verdict if he keeps his mouth shut!'

'Tsk, tsk,' the A.C. said. 'A mere technicality, Gently. I assume you are still interested in villains getting their deserts? Anyway, that's what you'll do.'

'I'll suggest a confession. No more.'

'And I trust you'll get it, with your ability. My best men usually get results.'

Gently left the phone-box without his smile and stood glowering some moments at the kerbside. The A.C. had come back very neatly – Gently really should have foreseen that one! Not that Fazakerly was likely to confess, either under pressure or treachery, but it was a stinging *quid pro quo* and the A.C. was probably still chuckling.

Gently got in the Sceptre, his current enthusiasm, and belted away with a surge of gas. Outside a café two streets away he spotted a parking-space, and slammed into it under the bumper of a Mark 10 Jaguar.

'You're not still kicking it around are you?'

He was alone with Fazakerly in the interrogation room. Reynolds, who'd brought Fazakerly in, had caught a stony glance and had hastily bowed himself out of the presence. Fazakerly was looking sprucer, more wholesome. They'd fetched him some clothes from the flat. He'd shaved, and the abrasion across his forehead was covered with a strip of pink plaster. His eyes were still ringed and looking tired but now there was more life in them. His suit was expensive. He wore a Yacht Club tie of dark blue silk, perfectly knotted.

'Take a seat,' Gently said.

'But I thought you'd washed your hands of me. You should, you know. I'm a lost soul. It's really not worth your wasting time on me.'

'All the same, I'm doing just that.'

'I should never have come to you in the first place.'

'But you did.'

'Yes, and now I feel bad about it. I'd sooner you forgot the whole thing.'

'Just sit down.'

Fazakerly sat. He had a feline grace of movement. In the suit he appeared more slender and it revealed an elegant slope of the shoulder. Colour had returned to his sallow cheeks and the absence of fuzz hardened his jaw-line. He had curious, fine-boned, bred-out good-looks of the sort which other men find irritating. His assurance had returned.

'Did you know they haven't charged me?'

'Don't pin any hopes on that,' Gently grunted.

'Oh, I don't. I haven't any hopes. I know they're only digging my grave a bit deeper.'

'So what are you pleased about?'

'I'm damned if I know. I'm feeling a tremendous sense of release. It's as though – yes, that's it! – as though I'm being reborn. And all that's happened is I've killed my wife.'

'You – did kill her?' Gently said.

'Yes. I mean, as far as everyone knows. They think I did it, which amounts to the same thing. When they look at me they see a wife-killer.'

'And that gives you release?'

'I can't describe it. You'd need my background to understand. To have been a worthless, degraded bum without a shred of self-respect. And then suddenly you're not a bum, it's all forgotten and swallowed up, you're someone different, a wife-killer, and that's the only way people think of you. Can't you see that? I suddenly don't care. Or rather, I want to go on being that thing.'

'You didn't want to go on being it this morning.'

'Not this morning. I was scared stiff. When you can see your life about to come apart you grasp at anything, like a drowning man. But even then I could see there was no hope, I mean of holding the bits together. Only just at that moment I was scared. I didn't have the nerve to let go.'

'And now you're content to be a wife-killer.'

'Better than that. I don't care.'

'In that case, you may as well confess.'

'It doesn't matter. They're sure I did it.'

Gently stared at him blankly. 'All right,' he said. 'You can smoke. I suppose the new Fazakerly does smoke?'

'I've got the feeling I can do anything.'

Reynolds had evidently leant over backwards to bend the rules for Gently's protégé, for Fazakerly immediately produced a full cigarette-case and a gold-plated lighter. He offered the case to Gently. Gently quickly shook his head. Fazakerly sprang a light and lit his cigarette carefully.

'You know, if you're still trying to help me,' he said, 'don't bother. I don't want to be helped any more. I'm not sure that anyone could help me. If I got off, if I had Clytie's money, I might drift back into being a bum. And just now I'm beyond all that. So let the balls run how they're played.'

'You'll like being a prisoner?' Gently said.

Fazakerly puffed and shook his head. 'It's so difficult to make you understand. You wouldn't believe me if I said I looked forward to it. You see, it's not a prison, not to me. I shall be sentenced to freedom. It's up till now I've been in prison, up till they fetched me away from your office. I was a prisoner in myself, a terrible solitary confinement, and I could see them coming to open the door and I was frantic to stop them doing it.

It was you who kicked me through that door. You were the last thing I was clinging to. But you broke the hold and kicked me out, and suddenly I was outside the prison. Because you don't think I'm innocent, do you?'

Gently shrugged, watching him curiously.

'No, you don't. And that was the kick. When I knew that, I simply stopped struggling.'

'You're in a state of shock, Fazakerly. It won't seem the same later on.'

'You can't see it. This isn't hysteria, my mind is quite as calm as yours is.'

'You know what your sentence would be, do you?'

'Fourteen years, less remission.'

'So you may be fifty before you come out.'

'But – how can I put it? – that doesn't signify!' He leaned forward on the table. 'You *must* see it: I'm a free person. Whether I'm quarrying stone on Dartmoor or sailing down-Channel I'm equally and inalienably free. You can't do anything to me. What I am you can't lock up. I've escaped. It's all the same. I just let go, and I was free.'

'You won't find any women in Dartmoor.'

Fazakerly shook his head. 'You're still not with me. And anyway, I never really wanted women. It was just compulsive, just pacing the cell.'

'Prisons smell. They're not pleasant places.'

'Did you sniff around in the flat?'

'You'll find the life there degrading.'

'I'll find life. The rest is words.'

'So if you're looking forward to it so much, what's the point of giving us trouble? Why not confess?'

'Because I didn't do it. And I'd simply rather not tell a lie.'

Gently drew a deep breath. 'Right,' he said, 'you didn't do it. And if you didn't do it, it's still up to us to find the person who did. And you can't mind us doing that, even though it dashes your prospects of Dartmoor, because on your own admission it's the same to you whether you're breaking stones or off on a spree. So perhaps you'll come to earth for a moment and try to give us some assistance.'

Fazakerly shrugged his neat shoulders. 'I certainly owe you something,' he said. 'And you've every right to be annoyed with me. This must be very awkward for you.'

'First, I'm not happy with the quarrel you had with your wife. There's something about it doesn't ring true. Half an hour earlier she was in a good mood and thinking only about dresses.'

Fazakerly smiled faintly. 'That sounds like Clytie,' he said. 'She spent the best part of her life chasing fashion trends. And mannequins.'

'But when you came in she was in a rage.'

'She was in a filthy temper. She was sitting there working it up, ready to clobber me when I walked in.'

'And about this Rochester woman – nothing else?'

'She was the text of the sermon.'

'Then what could have happened during the previous half-hour to put her into that temper?'

Fazakerly shook his head. 'She could flare-up in a moment,' he said. 'But this wasn't that sort of row, it was something she had on the boil. I don't know. I'm puzzled too. She was really putting the boot in. This whole business has just suddenly exploded without a reason, out of nowhere.'

'She couldn't have found something, perhaps – say some letters from Miss Johnson?'

'Sarah never wrote me letters. I used to ring her each day.'

'You can't explain it?'

'I'm sorry.'

'I'd like you to think back very carefully.'

'I'm afraid it's no use.'

'What I want you to remember is whether you and your wife were certainly alone in the flat.'

Fazakerly's mouth opened, then he hesitated. He gave Gently a quick look. 'That's odd,' he said. 'It's just possible you've put your finger on it there. I've gone over that scene a hundred times and each time it bothered me somehow. It may be you've found the answer. Though I didn't hear or see anyone.'

'Did you notice if any doors were open?'

'The door of the lounge, that was open. I dumped my kit in the hall and went straight in to get a drink.'

'Was that the only room you visited?'

'Yes. And I never got the drink.'

'What was your wife doing?'

'Just sitting.'

'With a cigarette?'

'She didn't smoke.'

He slapped his forehead. 'That's it!' he cried. 'She

didn't smoke – never has done. But the room was smoky when I went in. Somebody was there, or had been there.'

'It's a thin clue,' Gently grunted.

'But I noticed – I was going to make a remark. Then she started on me and I forgot it. It's bloody true – can't you believe me?'

'Who did you think might have been there?'

'Sybil of course. Who else?'

'I'm asking you.'

'Well I thought Sybil. And that's the reason for her going at me.'

'How do you mean?'

'It wasn't natural, not her threatening me about Sarah. I've had women all over the option and Clytie didn't care a damn. But suppose it was Sybil put her up to it – she hates my guts, you know that? – and suppose she was listening round the corner: then it begins to make sense. Clytie was laying on an act. She was showing Sybil how she could handle me, how I'd jump when she cracked the whip, even give up the woman I was mad about. Oh yes, it falls together all right. Put Sybil in there and it clicks.'

'But you didn't actually see Sybil.'

'Who the devil else could it have been?'

'Another smoker.'

'It took Sybil. She's the only one Clytie would want to impress.'

'And then, of course, after you'd left . . .'

'She killed her. That has to follow. I know it's illogical as hell, but it's the way it must have been.'

Gently frowned at Fazakerly's cigarette, which was burning unnoticed between his fingers.

'You know about the wills?' he asked.

'I do now, but I didn't when I made my statement.'

'Would you say there was a motive there?'

Fazakerly flicked the cigarette. 'It's tempting, isn't it?' he said. 'It would wrap it up for you nicely. But no, I can't suspect Sybil of that, malignant bitch though she is.'

'Your wife was worth a lot of money.'

'But Sybil's worth a lot more. And honestly, I have to say this, Sybil doesn't have a passion for the stuff.'

'So why should she want to kill your wife?'

'She wouldn't. I've said so all along.'

'But now you're suggesting that she did.'

Fazakerly slowly shook his head.

'Tell me about your wife and Mrs Bannister,' Gently said. 'What sort of relation was it they had: who was the dominant one, for instance, who used to lay down the law.'

'Have you talked to La Bannister?'

Gently nodded.

'Well, you may have got the wrong impression. She was the masculine element all right, but she never dominated Clytie. Clytie always had the edge. She could make Sybil shrivel up. She liked Sybil to wear the jack-boots because it titillated her, but she always had Sybil under control.'

Was your wife masochistic?'

'When it suited. She was anything that gave her an emotional kick. That was her preoccupation in life, raising a high emotional head of steam. Sybil was really a foil for Clytie, though it seemed to be Sybil who made the running. Sybil is a sadist, period. Twisting the knife gives her a thrill.'

'Was she jealous of your wife?'

'That's an understatement. They're worse than men, you know, are Lesbians.'

'And your wife of her?'

'Clytie too. They nearly broke up over one of the girls.'

He sent a curious look at Gently.

'You know what I'm talking about?' he said. 'A pair like La Bannister and my wife always have a third girl in tow. She'd be a mannequin, probably, or some hanger-on in that racket. You'd be surprised if you knew the extent of the Lesbian colony in London. Well, these girls come and go. They're just to freshen-up the scene. But Sybil got stuck on one once, and then the fur began to fly. She worked for a fashion magazine, this girl, and Clytie pulled some dirty tricks on her; she lost her job and her reputation. She was sunk without trace.'

'What was her name?'

'Oh . . . Beryl something.'

'Beryl Rogers?'

'That could be it.' His eyes opened a little wider. 'You do your homework, don't you?' he said.

'What happened to her?' Gently asked.

'I've no idea. She ceased to be.'

'What magazine was she on?'

Fazakerly's hand jerked a gesture.

'You see, I wasn't much around when the girls were in session. As the joker said, things like that can harm a young lad. I'd be out on the town following my own sexual pattern, which was probably no nicer though more socially acceptable. So I never met Beryl Rogers.'

'But she was dropped by Mrs Bannister.'

'Naturally. Her name was never mentioned again.'

'And it was the only trouble of that kind.'

'After that the girls were strictly temporary. Apart from Albertine, of course, who was a hired hand and didn't count.'

Gently silently nodded. Fazakerly dipped his cigarette in an ashtray.

'But this half-sister,' Gently mused, 'where does she come into it?'

'Brenda Merryn?'

'Brenda Merryn.'

Fazakerly went on tamping out the cigarette-end. At last he said.

'She was my little comfort. I slept with her more than with anyone.'

He ground the butt to pieces methodically, spreading shreds of tobacco over the ashtray. Then without looking at Gently he continued:

'Brenda was sorry for me, that's about it. I was such a weak and depraved devil, without a friend to my name, and no more backbone than a tadpole. So Brenda Merryn took pity on me.'

'Did your wife know that?'

'She either knew or suspected. She flung it up at me

a few times when she wanted to be catty. But Brenda still used to call round, Clytie never made an issue of it. She'd no use for me herself and Brenda was welcome to her leavings. In fact, Brenda was always welcome to the leavings. Clytie used to pass on surplus clothes to her. I figured in about the same category, some evening wear she'd got tired of.'

'How long was Miss Merryn your mistress?'

'Several years, off and on. But I never thought of her as my mistress. She was more like a sister with sex added.'

'You trusted her.'

'I could talk to her. She had no illusions about Clytie.'

'She was on good terms with your wife.'

'I suppose you could say that, in a poor-relation sort of way. She's' – he rocked his shoulders – 'she's a bit of a deep one. You always wonder about Brenda. I could never feel I was very close to her, though she was always on my side. That's what I mean when I say she was like a sister. She's family, but on her own.'

'Could you discuss your other affairs with her?'

'Why not? They were only a giggle.'

'You told her of Miss Johnson?'

'She knew about Sarah. Though I didn't blab too much in her case. Sarah is different, she's rather special; she's the woman I ought to have married. I suppose you always find them too late: that's the failing of monogamy.'

'And what was your answer to have been?'

Fazakerly shrugged. 'The bum's answer. Doing

nothing, living along with it. Till she got fed up and dropped me.' His eye caught Gently's. 'Look,' he said, 'for the last time – can't you see it? I don't give a damn what happens to me, but I'd like just one person to understand. I didn't kill Clytie. It's out of character. There's not enough bounce in me to do it. I'd just have toed the line and given up Sarah and boozed and slept it off with Brenda. That's me. I'm predictable. The bum line is my line.'

Gently nodded. 'Yes . . . predictable. People would know how you'd take it.'

'Ask anyone – even La Bannister. I haven't faced up to a problem for years. I know you can argue that I'm a weakling and that this is a weakling's way out, but I'm not just weak: I'm a bum too. That's the middle and crux of the business.'

'You'd have given her up and cried with Brenda.'

'Yes. Except I wouldn't have cried. And then I'd have settled to the round again, a naughty boy with his knuckles rapped.'

'And into this predictable pattern, you're saying . . .'

'I'm not saying anything. I'm taking it back. I can't believe such a thing of Sybil any more than I can of myself.'

'But that cigarette smoke was a fact?'

'So Sybil had been there. But she didn't do it.'

'Somebody did.'

'Put it down to a burglar.'

Gently stared at him and shook his head.

Fazakerly leaned back and sighed. 'All right,' he said. 'Have it your way. It probably makes the most sense, and it might as well be me who takes the rap. At least I'm getting something out of it. I've sloughed my old bumming skin. I'll be an aristocrat where I'm going: it's a sort of spiritual rags to riches.'

'And that's all you can say about it?'

'Yes. Stop wasting your time with me.'

'You could confess.'

'I could spit. But just now I haven't the energy.'

He gave Gently a hard look, and Gently grunted and rang the bell. He shoved his chair back and got up. Fazakerly followed him with his eyes. Then, when Gently had reached the door, he said:

'Will you be seeing Sarah at all?'

Gently stopped. 'And if I do?'

'Tell her I'm sorry. That's all.'

CHAPTER SIX

AFTER GREENWICH IT was a pretty smooth run through to Rochester, with the Sceptre slipping along at seventy for much of the way. The drive was soothing. Gently hadn't been out of town for a month, and the soft boom of the Rootes engine seemed to relax a tension. He was driving off the top and enjoying the sensation. Perhaps, except for the promise of this jaunt, he wouldn't have bothered about Sarah Johnson. At one moment was balanced in his mind the drab rush-hour plod home to Finchley and the straight stretches of the A2; and the A2 had won. And he was glad. The Sceptre felt good. It was handling like a surgical instrument. For a while it was even pushing to a distance the nagging conviction that he was making a fool of himself over Fazakerly . . .

Limit signs sprang upon him and he let the engine pull his speed down. The Sceptre crept through Strood and across the dull flood of the Medway. He turned down through the traffic about the Castle into the quieter waters of the Esplanade, and then left into a cul-de-sac bearing the name Vosper Gardens. He drove along it. Vosper Gardens was a road of slightly shabby detached houses. They were mid-Victorian in character and peered shyly from among mature trees and tall shrubs. At the top however, standing flush to the pavement, was a building which once perhaps had been a coach-house, a barn-shaped structure of red brick with a high roof of blue-black pantiles. It was presumably still in use as a store or garage, but at one end were two casement windows and a door. Gently coasted the Sceptre up to it and parked. At the slam of his door, pigeons rose.

He rang. There was movement inside but his ring was not directly answered. He had time to study the splines and bolt-heads of the door and the name, Parson's Mews, painted across it. Then the wrought-iron handle turned squeakily and he was faced by a brunette of about thirty.

'Miss Johnson?'

'Are you the police?'

'Chief Superintendent Gently. May I come in?'

Her face was pale and she stared uncertainly at him. No doubt he was not very welcome.

'It's . . . Johnny, of course?'

'Yes, John Fazakerly. I've just come away from talking with him.'

'Oh. He wouldn't – he didn't send a message?'

'A short message. Shall we go in?'

She stood aside from the door and admitted him to a little tiled hall. Then she opened a second door and they passed into a small sitting-room. It was a dull, ill-lighted room with few concessions to decoration; a framed Renoir print hung opposite the window and an Egyptian tapestry on another wall. A mahogany dining-table, too large for the room, was pushed up close to the window, and on it were spread the panels of a knitted garment and a paper covered with lines of pencilled figures. A painted book-case stuffed with paperbacks gave colour to a dark corner, and some miscellaneous chairs and a cottage settee made up the remainder of the furniture. It was dull; yet unexpectedly, it added up to something agreeable.

Sarah Johnson pointed to the table. 'I'm sorry if I kept you waiting,' she said. 'I was busy codifying a pattern. It's the way I make a living.'

Gently picked up one of the panels. 'You design these things?' he asked.

'Does it sound improbable? But yes, I design them. That's a mohair bolero for the winter collection.'

'It's very beautiful.'

'Thank you. I hope my customer thinks the same.'

'Who buys them from you?'

'Oh, mostly wool manufacturers. And I sell them to magazines, too.'

She was flushing. She turned away to straighten some items on the table, a pencil, a steel rule, a rounded block of india-rubber. She was slim in stretch slacks and an exquisitely-knitted sweater and her hair, which had a natural wave, swung forward about her face as she stooped.

'But . . . about Johnny. Oh, please sit down!'

She swept some papers from an easy-chair. Her

movements were quick and she wafted a sweet, fur-like odour from her person.

'I mean, is he all right? One hears so much . . .'

'He was quite cheerful when I left him.'

'It's so terrible. Do sit down! I feel I should be there trying to help him.'

Gently sat in the easy-chair and Miss Johnson perched on an arm of the cottage settee. It may have been accidental, but her face was turned from the direct light of the window. She had an oval face, slightly pointed, with a shapely nose and a small mouth, and her hands, clasped about her knee, were long-fingered with revealed bones.

'Are you . . . the other man was only a sergeant.'

'I'm not in charge of the case,' Gently said.

'But they've called you in.'

'Not even that. In fact, we're pretty well on the same side.'

'I don't understand!'

'Fazakerly came to me. My job is at New Scotland Yard. He turned himself in there this morning. He's a distant relative by marriage.'

'Related to you?'

'To my brother-in-law. I did meet him once, years ago.'

'Then you're – actually – helping him?'

Gently hunched a shoulder. 'I'm looking after his interests, you can say that. But don't misunderstand me, Miss Johnson, I'm not convinced of his innocence. And if I can help the prosecution to make their case, I'll be in duty bound to do it.'

Her eyes widened in the shadow. 'But,' she cried, 'he *is* innocent! You must know that if you've talked to him. Johnny wouldn't hurt anyone.'

'There's always a first time, Miss Johnson.'

'Not with Johnny. It's not possible.'

'Perhaps you don't altogether know him.'

'Oh, I do. Yes, I do.'

'Still, I'm not convinced myself, and I must make that plain. I'm willing to help him where I can, but first of all I'm a policeman.'

She slowly shook her head at him. 'Then you're doing nothing,' she said. 'If you don't believe him you won't help him. No, that's too much to expect. But he didn't do it for all that. I know, and nothing you say can alter it. It's his rotten wife who's at the bottom of it – I don't know how, but she is.'

'She didn't kill herself, Miss Johnson.'

'It was her rottenness that brought it about.'

'I'll give you that.'

'Her utter vileness. She was a devil. She deserved everything.'

'You knew her, then?'

'I? No! She never set foot in Rochester.'

'But you'd come into London, wouldn't you. To meet your editors, that sort of thing?'

Her hair swung. 'Yes, I do. But they're in the Street, not in Chelsea. Oh no, I heard all about her from Johnny: and that was enough, I can tell you.'

'Johnny may have been prejudiced.'

She twisted contemptuously. 'It's easy enough to say that. But you had only to see what she'd done to him to know what sort of a depraved bitch she was. Because Johnny's decent, that's the tragedy. He isn't what he'd have you believe. He's just been treated so badly so long that he's come to believe he's rotten himself. But I know him, and it's not so. And if you'd any perception you'd know it too. It's worse, it's the other way round, he's so damned nice at the bottom of him. The times are he's made me feel humble, he's basically more decent than I could ever be.'

'Yet you turned him down on Monday.'

'That. Yes. Yes, I did.' The colour flicked into her cheeks, too strong and sudden to be concealed. 'I turned him down. It wouldn't have worked. I knew it was a risk I had to take. If it was to be anything with us at all he had to be jolted into responsibility. It was a terrible temptation just to accept him – I wanted to, so much! – but I could see it would be a sort of betrayal, it would be letting the decent part of him down. After he'd gone I cried and cried. I thought perhaps I'd never see him again.'

'You nearly wouldn't have done,' Gently shrugged.

'Oh God. I know now what he did. But that was all right, he wouldn't have drowned. Johnny is safe enough at sea.'

'So it wasn't a pass at committing suicide.'

'Suicide? Oh, not Johnny!'

'If he'd left a murdered wife in London—'

'But it wasn't like that – it simply wasn't.'

The tangle of fingers clenched over her knee and she gave her hair a snatching toss. Light fell for a moment on her flushed face, revealing an almost childlike cast of feature. Then it was shadowed again.

She said carefully: 'Yes, he was in a state when he came back here on Monday. He was angry and desperate and talking wildly. He was trying to believe he would get a divorce. He knew his wife wouldn't divorce him but he thought he might manage to divorce her. He thought her relations with that other woman would outweigh anything alleged against him. It wasn't a trick. I know Johnny. As far as he knew, his wife was alive.'

'I see,' Gently said. 'Yet you mentioned none of this to Sergeant Buttifant.'

'Because he wasn't nagging me like you are. He was only asking a few questions.'

'He would ask what Johnny's state of mind was.'

'Yes, and I told him: he was upset. And I told him why, because of the row. And that Johnny had wanted to come and live with me.'

'But said nothing about him thinking his wife was alive.'

'No! I didn't see then how important it was.'

'What could be more important, Miss Johnson?'

She averted her head and said nothing.

'I'd like to get more into the picture,' Gently said. 'Such a lot is vague just at present. For instance, how did you come to meet Johnny? How long has the affair been going on?'

'I met him here. When he joined the Club.'

'You're fellow members?'

She shook her head. 'They use this building to store their gear. In the autumn. When they lay up.'

'But Johnny hasn't a yacht, has he?'

'He came to give the others a hand.'

'And you mix with them, do you? Know them well?'

'Naturally. I have to see something of them.'

'But Johnny attracted you.'

She stirred a little. 'I met him,' she said. 'That's all that matters. A year ago. He was unloading a trailer. I invited him in for a cup of tea.'

'Not knowing who he was?'

'I knew he was a member.'

'Not knowing his name?'

'How would I know that?'

'He was simply a stranger helping to unload a trailer, and you felt a compulsion to make his acquaintance.'

Her stare was not very friendly. 'Very well,' she said. 'I'd seen him there before. And yes, maybe I'd asked about him and knew his name. Perhaps it was I who made all the advances.'

'It was love at first sight.'

'Must you drag in that cliché?'

'I don't know,' Gently said. 'I was trying it for size. Or perhaps you were curious, say about his name. One doesn't often come across Fazakerly.'

She said nothing.

'Did you know that name?'

She gave a twist of her shoulders.

'By reputation perhaps – in your professional circle: the circle of magazines and fashion intelligence?'

She got down from the settee and went swiftly to the window, where she stood with her back to him, looking down the Gardens. In a small, dry voice she said:

'You've made your point then. Yes, I had heard of her. And I knew Beryl Rogers.'

Gently waited. Sarah Johnson continued for some while facing the window. She was resting her hands on the dining-table and rocking a little from one to the other. Overhead the pigeons had returned and their confused crooing sounded close and intimate, while an occasional car on the Esplanade made a distant buzz in passing. No clock was ticking. Perhaps it was this that gave the room such a hushed quality.

'Beryl Rogers was a special friend of mine.'

Now she came slowly back from the window. She sat down, this time upon the settee, her head and shoulders drooping forward.

'We were both about the same age. I met her at the school of journalism I attended. We both worked for the United Press group and we lived in a houseboat at Cheyne Steps. It was all very gay and very wonderful and we were both going to marry into Debrett.'

'Where is she now?'

Sarah Johnson shrugged. 'After the crash she went to New Zealand. There was nothing else for her to do. Clytie Fazakerly saw to that.'

'You've heard from her since?'

'A couple of times, but not for several years now. I expect she wanted to forget me, and I can understand that.'

'What exactly happened?'

'She was framed.'

'You mean that Mrs Fazakerly framed her?'

Sarah Johnson nodded. 'She planted a necklace on her, then had a C.I.D. man pick her up. There was a prosecution. Beryl got off. But she was finished in the Street. The Fazakerly creature cut a lot of ice there and Beryl lost her job and was blacked.'

'But why would Mrs Fazakerly do a thing like that?'

'Don't you know?'

'You tell me.'

'I only know what Beryl told me, but she had no reason to lie.' She hesitated, swinging her hair back. 'Beryl was an emotional person,' she said. 'Perhaps you can read between the lines. I don't find it easy to talk about this.'

Gently nodded.

'She met Sybil Bannister. It was at a private show of Louella Modes. She was there reporting with a staff artist, it was in the Blue Room at the Chat Noir. You perhaps don't know about that sort of thing, but it's a beastly sort of alcoholic hen-party, and most of them finish up a bit high and there's some odd behaviour goes on. Well, Sybil Bannister got a crush on Beryl, and Beryl was dozey enough to feel flattered. She let that woman take her home and she didn't come back to the houseboat. I'm not defending her, don't think that. She knew very well what she was in for. And she was weak enough to let it continue, I think she was even rather proud. Sybil Bannister is a remarkable woman in some ways and it was a kind of distinction to be her favourite.'

'And that's what she became?' Gently asked.

'Oh yes. Sybil Bannister was crazy about her. She bought her jewellery and clothes and took her round the smart places. She suggested Beryl should throw up her job and go and live with her in Paris. She was sweeping Beryl off her feet. I think she'd have done what Sybil Bannister wanted.'

'But then it all blew up in her face.'

'Yes. Exactly like that. Clytie Fazakerly came back from some holiday and the same evening Beryl was fixed.'

'How did she do it?'

'It was quite unsubtle. She gave a little supper in her flat. She was charming as an angel to poor Beryl and cooing and caressing to Sybil Bannister. She showed them some jewellery she'd brought back including a diamond and emerald necklace. When Beryl got back to the houseboat a detective was waiting for her. He found the necklace in her handbag.'

'But didn't Mrs Bannister stand by her?'

Sarah Johnson shook her head. 'Sybil Bannister left town. Beryl never saw her again. The case was thrown out at the Magistrates' Court because Clytie Fazakerly failed to appear. Perhaps she was afraid of what might have come out. But it was all the same to Beryl.'

'And so, because of this, she decided to emigrate.'

'She was completely bowled over. Clytie Fazakerly destroyed her, just as she was trying to destroy Johnny.'

'Johnny, whom you first met a year ago.'

Sarah Johnson said meekly: 'I'm not going to deny it. Yes, I had made enquiries about Johnny, and I knew very well who he was when I rubbed an acquaintance with him.'

She looked around her as though missing something, then sighed and closed her eyes a moment. Gently brought out a packet of cigarettes.

'Here,' he said. 'Have one of these.'

She raised her hand. 'Please don't tempt me. I'm trying to give them up. Again. But the habit rears its ugly head whenever I'm under nervous strain.'

'You've tried before, then?'

'I'm always trying, and this time I've gone nearly a month. But if I'm questioned by many more policemen I shall be back to forty a day.'

Gently shrugged and put the cigarettes away. 'I'm sorry,' he said. 'It's a policeman's function.'

'I know. I wasn't complaining about that. I'm just in a spot where a fag would count.'

She sighed again, then smoothed her hair and drew herself straighter.

'If you think I deliberately went after Johnny and seduced him,' she said, 'you'd be more or less right. I think that's what I had in mind, though it's hard to separate and label motives. They have a way of being something else which somehow won't go into words. But you may think the worst by all means. Let's say I wanted to seduce Clytie Fazakerly's husband. Not knowing, of course, he'd been seduced so many times that my poor effort was academic.'

'You felt it was revenge for what she'd done to Beryl.'

'Oh, and to me. I had a personal grudge. What happened to Beryl seemed to hit me too, it was like bad luck that rubbed off. First, I had to give up the houseboat. Then I lost my job with United Press. Then, I don't know, I was on a losing streak, I had a miserable affair with a married man. So all my bright promise had come to nothing and I slunk back home to lick my wounds. And I laid it at Clytie Fazakerly's door: Beryl in New Zealand, me in Rochester.'

'But you'd soon find out that Johnny was a womaniser.'

She winced. 'I'd rather you used a different word. It isn't true, either. He was driven that way. I trust him. I believe he's been faithful to me.'

'Does he know what made him attractive?'

'No.' Her eyes found his. 'And perhaps you'll be charitable enough not to tell him, especially since it's so different now. You see, I love Johnny. Like that. It doesn't matter why I picked up with him. In fact, it might have been the reason after all, with his being who he is a special bonus. I said it was hard to separate motives. But I love Johnny. And he loves me.'

'Then of course you'd have had some plans for him.'

'Plans?'

'If you'd loved him and he'd loved you. Carrying on as you were wasn't very satisfactory. Going shares with a yacht club in Johnny's weekends.'

'You're so complimentary, aren't you?' she said.

'Just constitutionally curious, Miss Johnson.'

'I'd say you were too cynical for your own good. But that's probably a policeman's function too.'

Gently hunched a shoulder. 'So what were your plans?'

'We didn't have any plans,' she said. 'I was just trying to build up Johnny's confidence, that was the only plan I ever had.'

'But where was that going?'

'Nowhere at all.'

'And nowhere at all was satisfactory?'

'I tell you,' she said, twisting, 'it was too impossible. There was nothing to be done while Johnny was down.'

'But perhaps you had thought a little beyond that, to the time when you'd put some stuffing in him, to the time when he might stand up to his wife: to the time, even, when he might be rid of her?'

'No, I didn't!'

'It didn't enter your thoughts?'

'Oh, God, yes, I thought about it, then! Yes, I thought about it, like a win on the pools or anything else that could never happen. But that's all I did. I thought about it.

'But never how it might be brought about?'

'A divorce. I dreamed of a divorce.'

'And nothing else?'

'I hoped the house would fall on her!'

She covered her face with her hands and gave a few moaning sobs, but they were over in a moment and she was facing him again, tearfully fierce.

'You don't mean that!' she cried. 'It's too ridiculous to take seriously.'

'What don't I mean, Miss Johnson?'

'That I – that I was a sort of Lady Macbeth! That I egged Johnny on to kill his wife, and hoped the fool would get away with it – or that the police would never guess. No – you can't be serious.'

'But that wasn't my meaning, Miss Johnson.'

'If it wasn't, what was?'

'I think you've guessed already. You had a vital stake in this business.'

'Me!' Her eyes expanded. 'No, this is just a bad joke. As though there were a way to drag me in, with all the nagging in the world.'

'For instance, Johnny left you here, and found you here when he returned. But I believe Sergeant Buttifant omitted to ask how you spent the time between.'

'And if I say I was in town you'll arrest me?'

'Were you in town, Miss Johnson?'

'Oh yes. I go there, you know. I had a lunch appointment with the editor of *Ton*.'

'On Monday?'

'On Monday. Now why don't you produce the hand-cuffs?'

Gently paused. There was a touch of virago in the way Sarah Johnson was glaring at him. Her head was drawn down on her shoulders and her small mouth was dragged.

'Well then,' he said. 'Perhaps you'll give me details. How do you make the journey to town.'

'I drive there. I'm not so impoverished that I can't afford a car. I left here at half past eleven and I was in Southampton Street at about a quarter to one. I met

Molly Steward, she's the fashion editor, and we had a pub lunch in the Prince of Wales. She was giving me the new line they're going to push this winter. And after that I ordered some wool at Mallenders' branch in the Strand. Then I pottered a bit round the shops. Then I drove back here.'

'When did you arrive?'

'Fivish.'

'So you were only just ahead of Johnny?'

'Oh, I haven't a leg to stand on. I drive a TR3, too.'

'How long were you pottering around the shops?'

'Over an hour. Nearly two. And I didn't meet anyone who would remember me, so I might just as well have been in Chelsea.'

'You had time to go there, Miss Johnson.'

'Yes. It's too perfect.'

'And you didn't go there . . . not perhaps to have an interview with Mrs Fazakerly?'

She stared at him, then laughed bitterly. 'You can work it all in, can't you?' she said. 'Just show you the hind-leg of a rabbit and already there's game-pie on the menu. But I'm not your game-pie, Superintendent. You'll have to make shift with poor Johnny. Because I was nowhere near Chelsea on Monday, and I certainly didn't interview Clytie Fazakerly.'

'Then why was she suddenly so inimical towards you.'

'Why?'

'Yes, why, Miss Johnson. That's the question. Apparently you were just another woman of Johnny's. Why weren't you ignored like all the others?'

Sarah Johnson got up. 'I don't know,' she said. 'And furthermore I don't care. It's because of nothing I've said or done to her, you can write that down in your note-book. And now if you don't mind, and if you're not arresting me, I've things to get on with.'

She went to the table and opened a drawer and took out a new twenty packet of Player's. She lit one and inhaled deeply. She drove a cloud of smoke towards Gently.

CHAPTER SEVEN

HIS RETURN TRIP was made with lights and with less bravura than the outward run. In town, the rush-hour jamming had eased again into a respite of semi-free movement. He drove through New Cross and Camberwell and crossed the river at Vauxhall Bridge. Outside Divisional H.Q. he parked in the V.I.P. slot, which the Sceptre was now clicking into as though it owned it.

'Sir.'

A uniformed man came over and saluted.

'Well?'

'A message from Inspector Reynolds, sir. He's been called out on the Fazakerly case, and he'd like you to wait for him if it's convenient.'

Gently stared at him. 'Where's the Inspector gone?'

'To Carlyle Court, sir. About half an hour ago.'

'What was he after?'

'He didn't say, sir.'

'Right,' Gently grunted. 'I'll be in his office.'

He went on up, yielding to a compulsion to flick

one of the rubber plants as he passed it, and let himself into the fluorescent brightness and bleak unhospitality of Reynolds' office. His eye searched for a palliative, and found an evening paper spread on the desk. He dumped himself down by it. The paper, predictably, was open at an account of Fazakerly's apprehension.

PENTHOUSE SLAYING HUSBAND FOUND

Walks Into Yard

Fazakerly Assists Police

John Sigismund Fazakerly, 38, husband of the woman whose battered body was found in a luxury flat in Chelsea, today walked into Scotland Yard and offered the Police his assistance. They had been searching for him since Monday when the body was found. He has been taken to Chelsea Police Station where he is helping the Police investigation. According to one source Fazakerly claims to have spent the past three days on a sea trip. A police spokesman said that an arrest was probable 'within the next few hours'.

Gently was mentioned cautiously as having visited Divisional H.Q. after the transfer, and Reynolds was pictured striding sharp-eyed down the steps of Carlyle Court. No picture of Fazakerly was apparently available. Instead they had one of the Murdered Woman. She was wearing a sack coat of two seasons ago and had a bemused, almost imbecile, expression. It had no hint of that strange nakedness which was the essence of her identity. She was merely another woman in another press picture, illustrating another story, by accident this one. Gently lit a pipe and smoked and stared at the vacuity of the picture.

Reynolds, when he returned, actually tapped at his own office door. He came in subduedly, followed by Buttifant, and was carrying a manilla envelope which bulged slightly.

'Sorry to keep you, Chief.'

Gently grunted. Reynolds took the chair reserved for visitors. He had an air of awkwardness about him, as though he had something unpleasant to get off his chest. He opened his mouth, changed his mind, then said at last in a hurry:

'Chief, I've come round to your point of view. I've decided not to charge Fazakerly.'

Gently's brows lifted. 'Come again?'

'I've decided we don't have a case. Not a case we could win, that is. So I've put a tail on him and let him go.'

'You've done what?'

'I couldn't hold him, not after I decided not to charge him.' He rustled the envelope nervously. 'I've been having a word with Macpherson,' he said.

Gently fumbled a light for his pipe. This wasn't what he'd expected at all! He had an uneasy sensation of having pushed too hard, and of now having the tables turned on him. Perhaps till now he'd failed to realize how strong was his conviction of Fazakerly's guilt: he'd counted on Reynolds to uphold it staunchly, even while he himself was flirting with doubts.

'Macpherson was here about another matter,' Reynolds explained. Macpherson was attached to the Public Prosecutor's office. 'I thought I'd ask him for an opinion. And you were right, Chief. He didn't like it. He said I'd better hang on for a bit and try to sew it up tighter. He didn't like Mrs Bannister for a witness. He seemed to think we were concentrating too hard on Fazakerly.'

'Macpherson,' Gently said. 'Yes . . . he's canny.'

'He took the same line as you did, Chief.'

'And so you let him go.'

'Isn't that what you'd have wanted?'

Gently shrugged. Now he wasn't so certain!

'But you had the sense to put a tail on him.'

Reynolds looked perplexed. 'Yes . . . I thought . . .'

'Where did he go?'

'At first to his sister-in-law's, then he took a room at the Coq d'Or in Vincent Street. He's in there now, having a meal. Thompson phoned a few minutes ago.'

'Have the Press got on to him?'

'Don't think so, Chief.'

'There'll be some pretty hot copy when they do.'

Reynolds squirmed. 'But I couldn't go on holding him. Macpherson said outright he wouldn't recommend the case. And anyway, I've come up with a new lead since then, and this one doesn't point to Fazakerly.'

He hastily jerked open his envelope and shot the contents on the desk.

What fell, or cascaded, from the envelope was a necklace composed of diamonds and emeralds.

* * *

It was an expensive necklace. It flashed and iridesced with a fire that was unmistakable, and the principal stones were of a size to silence deprecatory conjecture. They were set in baroque platinum settings dusted with chips and seed pearls, alternate diamonds and emeralds, in the form of a gorget linked with a chain. It was formidable. One knew at a glance it transcended the common extravagances of jewellery.

Gently gazed at it, lying tumbled on the desk.

'So,' he said, 'where did this come from?'

'It came from a dustbin.'

'From where?'

'From a dustbin. A dustbin in the back area of Carlyle Court.'

'Did it now,' Gently said. 'Well, I knew they were pretty well-heeled in that district. But if they're tossing this sort of thing in their dustbins there's going to be a rush to sign-on the dust-wagon. Who turned it in?'

'Old Dobson, the porter. He makes a point of sorting over the rubbish.'

'I'm not surprised. There's a future in it. And of course, this belonged to Mrs Fazakerly?'

Reynolds nodded. 'Dobson took it to Stockbridge, who got on the phone to us in a hurry. He knew who it belonged to because he used to keep it for her. There's a safe in his office where tenants deposit valuables. She had this out on the Monday morning ready for some function in the evening.'

'And it wasn't in the flat when you took over?'

'No. Buttifant and Thompson checked the flat.'

'There were some bits in a jewel-box, sir,' Buttifant said.

'But they're still up there. We've just had a look.'

'And the flat's been sealed.'

'You saw it was, Chief. Nobody's been monkeying there since. So this must have been removed prior to our going there, that is, between about noon and four-forty-seven p.m.

'Which irresistibly suggests that the murderer took it.'

'Well, yes, Chief, I think it does. An ordinary thief wouldn't have thrown it in the dustbin. It had to be someone who knew it was too hot.'

Gently picked up the necklace and let it run through his fingers.

'Odd,' he said. 'Fazakerly suggested a burglar. Yet a burglar doesn't fit any better than he does, because all a burglar had to do was to sneak out.'

'But if she caught him at it—'

'Sitting on the settee?'

'He may have been lurking on the veranda.'

'So why didn't he lurk there a bit longer, instead of murdering Mrs Fazakerly on his way out?'

'Well, he was in full view of the street—'

Gently clicked his tongue impatiently. 'And so he must have been for over an hour, from when Mrs Fazakerly came back from lunch. But he wouldn't have been there in the first place. You don't look for jewellery in the lounge. He'd have been frisking her dressing-room down the hall – that's where the jewel-box was, wasn't it?'

Reynolds nodded reluctantly.

'So that's where she'd trap him when she came back. And if he hadn't made his getaway sooner, he'd have done it while the row was going on in the lounge.'

'But then why did he get rid of the necklace, Chief?'

'That's my point. He doesn't fit.'

'But someone did—'

'Someone did. And I agree it doesn't point to Fazakerly.' He gave the necklace a little toss. 'Did you show this to Mrs Bannister?' he asked.

'No. Stockbridge identified it positively. I didn't see any need to bother her. You don't think . . .'

Gently hunched a shoulder. He laid the necklace back on the desk. For a few moments he sat silently studying it and teasing out its shape with a reverent forefinger. Then he said:

'Right. Get her on the phone, will you? Tell her you want her here for something important.'

Reynolds hesitated. 'We could soon run it round, Chief—'

'No.' Gently smiled. 'I think I'd like to have her here.'

She arrived. Reynolds had sent an Imperial for her, after much humility over the phone, but still she had kept them waiting and could be heard expostulating on her way up the stairs. She was wearing a green satin evening dress and a mink cape and elbow-length gloves and carried a snake-skin bag with a gold chain, gold frame and jade studs. She swept into the office, then saw Gently.

'Oh,' she said. 'You're behind this, are you? I might have guessed it needed someone with less consideration than Inspector Reynolds.'

Gently inclined his head.

'And since I'm here, I may as well tell you that I'm furious. You've let Siggy loose. And I won't stand for it. If you don't prosecute him, I will.'

'You know about that, Mrs Bannister?'

'Yes. The Merryn woman phoned me. And I'm fairly certain of one thing, Superintendent, that it was your meddling that was responsible. I think it's scandalous. I intend to complain, and if I can show you up I will. There's too much softness with murderers these days, not to mention very peculiar police action.'

'Miss Merryn rang to tell you we'd released Fazakerly?'

'She certainly did. I suppose it's true?'

'She told you she'd seen him?'

'Of course. She was shocked. I believe she was concerned for her personal safety.'

'Why should she be, Mrs Bannister?'

'Oh, don't pretend to be dense. He thinks it was she who told Clytemnestra about the woman, and knowing her I would say he's right.'

'Did she say he'd threatened her?'

'Not exactly that. But if he's done it once he can do it again. The more so because he seems to be getting away with it this time, thanks to interference from a certain quarter. Now perhaps you can tell me why I'm wanted?'

Gently nodded. 'Won't you sit down, Mrs Bannister.'

'First I'd like to know why I'm here.'

'It's because of some special knowledge we think you have.'

She stared hard for a moment, then looked about for the chair. Reynolds, who'd been listening unhappily to these exchanges, hastened to slide the chair towards her. She laid her bag on the desk but didn't take off her gloves. She sat sedately, ankles crossed, skirt arranged and hands together.

'Well?'

'Do you remember a Beryl Rogers?'

That was the last question she'd expected. Her eyes widened and then blurred, and a gloved hand twitched towards her bosom. But she said icily:

'Am I supposed to?'

'I'm asking you, Mrs Bannister.'

'Very well then. Yes, I remember her. I remember a Beryl Rogers.'

'She was a friend of yours.'

'Not exactly a friend, just a very brief acquaintance. A few weeks. I know nothing about her. It was several years ago.'

'You've lost sight of her completely.'

'Yes, completely. She went abroad.'

'She hasn't, to your knowledge, returned to this country?'

Her eyes jumped to his. 'No. Not to my knowledge.'

'Would she have contacted you if she had?'

She shook her head slightly, eyes still fixed on him.

'But you were an acquaintance of hers, you could

probably have helped her. I mean, you might have contacts that would help her professionally.'

She shook her head again. 'No. I couldn't have helped her. And she wouldn't have come after help. I'm sorry, I can't give you information about her. She simply went abroad about five years ago.'

'Did you know the friend she was living with?'

Mrs Bannister said sharply: 'What friend?'

'Another journalist. A Miss Johnson. They were sharing accommodation at the time you knew her.'

Mrs Bannister's eyes glinted. 'No, I didn't know her. Beryl never mentioned a friend to me. She was living in a houseboat down at the Steps, a frightful old wreck. I never went aboard it. Who told you about the friend?'

'You don't know who she is?'

'Haven't I already said so?'

'Or that she lives in Rochester?'

Mrs Bannister went still. 'Not – Siggy's woman?' Gently nodded.

'Oh my God.' Mrs Bannister paled, and this time her hand reached her bosom. She stared haggardly at nothing and rocked a little in her chair.

'Perhaps now you appreciate our interest,' Gently said. 'There's an unusual connexion here with Mrs Fazakerly. And if by chance Miss Rogers has returned to this country we shall be very interested to interview her.'

Mrs Bannister closed her eyes. 'What a mess,' she said.

'Is that all you have to tell us?'

'Beryl isn't mixed up with it. She's in New Zealand. She'd never have come back over here.'

'You're quite certain.'

'Yes.'

'It wasn't the reason why Mrs Fazakerly was angry.'

'No! It couldn't have been.'

'Nor, for example, why this was taken from the flat?'

She stared at his slowly-opening hand and at the necklace lying in it. She caught her breath and made a trembling gesture. She was paler than before.

Reynolds also was gaping big-eyed, though not, in his case, at the necklace. Quite apparently the Beryl Rogers angle was fresh ground to him. Gently had produced it, like a conjurer's silks, from nothing accountable or consequent, and the reaction to it of Mrs Bannister was proof enough of its validity. But where, how, could he have come by this draft of seeming omniscience?

'Well, Mrs Bannister?'

'It's . . . Clytemnestra's necklace.'

'You have no doubt of that?'

She shuddered. 'None. I know it too well. I know it better than anything of mine.'

'Because Mrs Fazakerly was always wearing it?'

'Because, yes, she was always wearing it. Whenever we went anywhere together she wore that necklace. It was a symbol.'

'A symbol of what?'

'Of domination. Of triumph. Of threat. In one word, of her power. Of the power she had to destroy people.'

'And she wore it for your benefit?'

'Entirely for my benefit.'

'She had the power to destroy you?'

Mrs Bannister shuddered again, and said 'Yes.'

'So,' Gently said, 'you went in fear of her.'

But now she shook her head vigorously. 'No. I loved her, you understand? And she loved me, in her own fashion. I loved her even because she wore the symbol, because she had that power over me; it was right, it belonged to her, she had the prerogative of life or death. But I see you don't understand, and perhaps it's impossible that you should. You are mere men, and your love is egotism. The esoteric side is beyond you.'

'Perhaps you thought she wouldn't have destroyed you.'

'Quite the contrary. I believed she would. Every loving is a destruction and without it is no love. She destroyed me once and made me live again. The knife of destruction was always pricking me. The sublime of love lies in that knife-point and the belief in the thrust which doesn't come.'

'But the knife slipped a little with Beryl Rogers.'

'The knife destroyed me. It was intended.'

'And destroyed her.'

'She came between us. I know that now. Clytemnestra was right.'

She leaned back with closed eyes, her pale face dragged and flat.

'Clytemnestra was in part to blame,' she said. 'She would go over to Paris alone. She had a friend there, I don't doubt, or some hireling who pleased her. I've never stood in Clytemnestra's way. I loved her too much for petty jealousy. But I missed her, that was what led to it, I was so miserable and lonely; and then I saw Beryl wearing a green costume, and something snapped, and I knew it must be. I made her drunk and took her home and the poor slut was almost grateful. And I was blind with infatuation. I even put some of Clytemnestra's clothes on her. Oh, I committed every blasphemy; when Clytemnestra came, the knife went home.'

'In effect, Miss Rogers was falsely accused.'

'I don't know what happened. I was sent away.'

'You know what part this necklace played in it.'

'Yes. I had to know why Clytemnestra wore it.'

'And you have no more feelings for Beryl Rogers, Mrs Bannister?'

'No more feelings. That self was destroyed.'

'So if I rang this bell and she walked through the door, you would scarcely bother to turn your head.'

Her eyes sprang open, but she didn't turn her head. She glared at Gently. 'Very well,' she said. 'You have found the necklace, and you know what it means. Am I permitted to know where you found it?'

'Don't you know already, Mrs Bannister?'

'Is that what you think?'

Gently said nothing.

'That I – that I took the necklace from Clytemnestra – and killed her – because – because . . . ?'

Their eyes held for a moment silently.

'Yes,' she said, 'you do think it! And you're right to

think it, because it's so credible. So inexorably credible.'

'Did you take the necklace?' Gently asked.

'Yes. In dreams a hundred times. And the dividing line is so thin, isn't it, between reality and dreams. So perhaps I did take it in reality, though it seems to me like a dream; and the rest of it too, I may have dreamed that, or it may have been real, and I killed Clytemnestra. But it's a vivid dream, if it's a dream, and I can see it must be convincing – much more convincing, for instance, than that poor weak Siggy should ever nerve himself to homicide.'

Gently sighed. 'Mrs Bannister,' he said, 'did you in fact take the necklace?'

'In fact?'

'In fact.'

'No, Superintendent. You will hardly believe me, but I didn't.'

'Did you see it at any time on Monday?'

'I saw her with it before lunch. I went to fetch her down to cocktails. She was just unwrapping it from the tissue.'

'Where did she put it?'

'In her jewel-box, which is on the dressing-table in the dressing-room. She toyed a little with it first. She always liked me to see her handling it.'

'What time was that?'

'Ten minutes to one.'

'Did she lock the box?'

'Its lock is broken. She may have locked the flat when we went down. It has a spring dead-lock on the door.'

'Who has a key for it?'

'Siggy, myself. I don't think Mrs Lipton has one. But that's not very important, is it? Siggy wasn't there, and I was with Clytemnestra.'

'You didn't dream of an excuse for stepping out during lunch.'

She closed and opened her eyes. 'I was serving lunch, remember? And I was already dreaming of going back with her and killing her. Slipping out for the necklace would have been superfluous.'

'So who do you think took it?'

'Is a burglar too banal?'

Gently nodded. 'Not inexorably credible.'

'Well, it wouldn't have been Siggy, I don't believe that either. Nor Mrs Lipton. So it has to be me.'

'But suppose Beryl Rogers was back in London?'

Mrs Bannister shivered. 'No, she'd never have come back here. Besides, after five years it's too improbable. She'll have married some sheep-farmer and be having ten kids.'

'She had a big score to settle with Mrs Fazakerly.'

'But the improbability! She has nothing to do with it.'

'To her, the necklace was more than a necklace.'

'Nothing will convince me. The idea is too horrible.'

'Then what is the alternative, Mrs Bannister?'

She stared at him with desperation. 'Me, of course. I'm the alternative, the perfect and only convincing answer. You won't have Siggy now, will you? Not with this necklace turning up where it shouldn't! Oh,

I can see why you let him go, especially when you'd dug up the story about Beryl.'

She jumped to her feet.

'Are you going to detain me?'

Gently shook his head. 'But you could be more helpful.'

'Helpful! I'm admitting I must have done it.'

'That won't do. Without some details.'

'So who will you arrest, if not me, not Siggy, and with Beryl Rogers in New Zealand?'

Gently shrugged. 'The murderer, I hope.' He picked up the necklace. 'And the thief.'

When she had gone Reynolds turned to Gently.

'Chief,' he said, 'this is going too fast. Nobody mentioned a Beryl Rogers to me. I've a feeling I'm being left down the line.'

Gently grinned. 'Perhaps you should have asked Fazakerly.'

'Yes – but where did I get my questions?'

'You went to Brenda Merryn for those.' Gently paused. 'Though I'm still wondering why she made me a present of them.'

He ran over his information to Reynolds, who sat listening with silent attention. At last the C.I.D. man said:

'Then I wasn't so crazy when I let Fazakerly loose.'

'He isn't off the hook yet,' Gently said. 'But the case against him is looking sick. Unless this necklace being stolen is a coincidence there's a chance we were wrong about him.'

'We could make a case against Mrs Bannister.'

'Macpherson wouldn't like that either. A case with two suspects, equally hot, is a prosecutor's nightmare. But then there's Miss Johnson and Brenda Merryn. And a whiff of sulphur from New Zealand. And even Stockbridge down in the basement: he may have taken a fancy to this bauble.'

'We checked his alibi. He's clear.'

'He'd have a master-key to the flat. But what I'm getting at is there are too many cases against too many people, and somehow . . . it smells.'

'How do you mean, Chief?'

'I'm not sure. It's just a hunch grumbling in my belly. Too much colour, too much decoration, and perhaps something very simple behind it. Maybe I'll see it when I've slept on it. But as of now, it's a smell.'

He lit his pipe and blew rings into the conditioned sameness of the office air. Reynolds gazed at them frowningly and dug in his pocket for some form of confection.

'So what will I do, Chief?' he said.

'You'll find Beryl Rogers,' Gently said. 'Sarah Johnson says she has family in Worcester, so you can make a start there. Then check with the United Press, where she used to work, and the New Zealand Office in the Haymarket, and the Immigration Office. Find where she went to, if she came back, where she is now.'

'What about Fazakerly?'

'Take your man off. He won't stray far from his

money. You made him rich when you didn't charge him. He'll be on to his lawyers tomorrow.'

He blew more rings.

'Yes,' he said. 'You changed the direction of quite a sum.'

CHAPTER EIGHT

IT WAS AFTER nine when he garaged the Sceptre at 16 Elphinstone Road, but Mrs Jarvis, his 'jewel', had a mixed grill waiting for him on the hotplate. He ate it in the den and drank some rough red wine along with it, propping the late editions around him on cruet, tea-pot and fruit-bowl. This was his habit in the evening, whether the meal was at six or midnight. From his particular problems he withdrew into the wider world reflected here. It was not escape, since his own problems were an aspect of the panorama, but a change of view, a standing back to merge the trees with the wood. The papers gave him a reference, a monitor glance at all cameras. He ate, drank, read and stood at one again with his world.

When Mrs Jarvis had cleared away he selected and filled a large bent pipe, then went to his shelves and after a search located Andre Maurois' *Quest for Proust.* Yes, Illiers was Combray. It was a small market town near Chartres. Only a short step from Paris, a step easily taken by an Albertine. A girl of poor family, no doubt, with few prospects in her home town, but with a sturdy pulchritude that would have its value in the great city a few miles distant. How had Clytie Fazakerly and La Bannister picked her up? In the regular way, through an employment agency? In a café on the Left Bank or in Montmartre? At some special establishment catering for Lesbians? He grunted, put the book away and picked up the one he was currently reading. No more of Fazakerly till the morning! At least, the fellow was sleeping outside a cell.

But he'd barely sat down in his consecrated chair when the phone rang on his desk. He went to it and jerked it up with loathing, ready to jump down somebody's throat.

'Is that you, George?'

The voice was his sister's.

'George, I can't talk for very long. Geoffrey didn't want me to ring you at all, but I felt I must . . . he's in the study with someone.'

Gently lapsed into the desk chair. 'It's about young Fazakerly, is it?' he growled.

'Yes, Johnny Fazakerly. We know him, George, he's a nephew of Aunty May Fazakerly's. And in the paper tonight . . . well, there were headlines. He's local, of course. That makes it news.'

Gently grimaced. 'It's news, period.'

'But George, what's happening? Did he do it?'

'It wouldn't surprise me.'

'George, how terrible. I mean, someone we know . . . actually a relative.'

Gently swivelled the chair a degree and fixed his

gaze on the stuffed pike. He liked his sister, but there were times when dear Bridget jarred with him a little. To her he was still a small boy playing wilful and incomprehensible games . . .

'He gave himself up to me this morning,' he said.

'What . . . ?'

'Walked into my office. Gave himself up. Said he wanted me to believe in his innocence because the facts were all against him.'

'Poor Johnny! What did you do?'

'Handed him over, what else? He was right about the facts, and I'm not prescient. So over to Chelsea he had to go.'

'But . . . couldn't you do anything to help him, George?'

'Oh yes. I could pull my rank on the officer in charge. And as a result I've gummed-up a perfectly good case and perhaps robbed a deserving spinster of a fortune.'

'But what about Johnny?'

'He's free as the air. He's living it up at a swish hotel.'

'You mean you've got him off, George?'

'He's out for the moment.'

'Oh George, that's wonderful!'

'So happy you think so.'

He sneered at the pike, which sneered back. It was a twenty-four pounder, caught in Norfolk. Perhaps it didn't much resemble his sister Bridget, but just now it pleased him to imagine a likeness.

'George?'

'Yes.'

'You didn't know his wife, did you?'

'I'm getting to know her. Little by little.'

'She was a bitch, George. I don't like saying it, but she deserved whatever happened to her. You know how she got her money, don't you?'

'Fazakerly told me.'

'And that isn't all. She used to have relations with other women. She was expelled from school for that sort of thing.'

'How do you know?'

'You forget she's local. She went to Ferndale Grammar School with Charlotte Manners. There was a business there with one of the mistresses – another bitch. A Sybil someone.'

'A Sybil someone?' Gently came alert.

'Yes, Sybil . . . Tremaine, that's the name. She lost her job, but it didn't matter. Her family have money and she married well. But Clytie was funny, George, that's the point. I'm sure poor Johnny went through hell. He was silly to marry her, but she was quite a good-looker, and she was rich, of course. But it wasn't worth it.'

'I'm sure poor Johnny is agreeing with you. Who did Sybil Tremaine marry?'

'What . . . ? Just a minute, George, let me listen. I think it's Geoffrey coming out . . .'

'Was it a Fletcher Bannister?'

'Yes, that's right. He was killed in a road smash, remember? George, I must hang up . . . and George, thank you! I knew you wouldn't let me down.'

Her phone descended; but not before Gently had heard Geoffrey's interrogative bass off-stage.

After the call he sat some minutes still exchanging glances with the pike. So the Fazakerly–Bannister relation went back further than its blossoming at Carlyle Court! Around twenty years ago it must have begun, in that select school near Taunton, which he had once visited with Geoffrey and Bridget to watch their niece receive her prizes. And La Bannister had been a teacher there (yes, that sorted with her bearing!), a young graduate, as she must have been, from one of the senior universities; and Clytie, Clytemnestra, her maiden-name unknown, sixteen, seventeen, eighteen years old, in the salad-days of her disturbing beauty. How had it gone? At first discreetly, a furtive crush on both sides; with Clytie, probably already an initiate, making the running from the start. Then it developed and became bolder, with the inevitable arrogance of a Lesbian relationship, till, after warnings and lectures, the crash came, and Ferndale purged itself of the sinners. What followed? Trouble at home. Clytie would behave like a caged tigress. Her step-father, Merryn, would be only too happy to find someone to take her off his hands. And sooner or later, probably sooner, she had gravitated to the care of a lecherous relative – though a rich one, it went without saying – and finally to independence and marriage. Meanwhile her partner in crime had retired to the shelter of her well-to-do family, and had also become rich. And, in a way not dissimilar.

Gently stared very hard at the pike. Was the pattern

coincidental? Both these women had attached themselves to rich, elderly men, who had not for long troubled them by continuing in the world. Then they had come together again, enriched by the spoils of the beasts; Clytie, certainly, with the foolishness of a husband, but with only enough of one to make them sport. And how had the beast-providers died? One, at all events, in a road smash. And a road smash was simple enough to engineer if one brought a modest intelligence to the problem . . .

He took the phone again and began to dial, but was interrupted by the entry of Mrs Jarvis.

'Sorry to trouble you, Mr Gently,' she said. 'But there's a woman downstairs asking to see you.'

He laid the phone down. 'Who is it?'

'She wouldn't give her name, Mr Gently.'

'Then tell her—' he began, and stopped.

For Brenda Merryn stood in the doorway.

The den was illuminated by a reading-lamp and Mrs Jarvis made a silent comment. On going out she switched on the room-light and paused with her fingers on the switch. Then she went.

Brenda Merryn winked at Gently. 'I don't think your good lady trusts us.'

She went deliberately back to the door and switched the room-light off again.

'All right with you?'

Gently hunched a shoulder. Brenda Merryn came back into the room. She was dressed to kill in a plunging gown of crimson *crépe* with a frilled bosom.

Over this she was wearing a black three-quarter coat, but now she slipped it off and threw it over a chair. She stood hands-on-hips, smiling down at Gently, pervading the den's pipe-smoke with Blue Grass.

'Like me?'

She swung her hips.

'I'm a dangerous woman when I'm roused. Your Mrs Mop was quite right. Nobody would believe I'm here to talk ballet.'

'So why are you here?'

'Seduction, perhaps. You annoyed me so much this afternoon. But you were on duty this afternoon, so you had to be strong and incorruptible, didn't you? Only now you're not on duty. You're just a man. In a room. With a woman.'

'I wouldn't rely on me not being on duty.'

She gave a laugh. 'That would be too dull. If policemen were always, but always, policemen, and never did anything about pretty girls. She wasn't your wife, was she?'

'That was Mrs Jarvis.'

'You're not married, engaged, emotionally involved?'

He shook his head.

'So what's wrong with me? We're free and white, so why not be friends?'

'And that's your only reason for coming here?'

She gave a twirl. 'I thought it was a good one. You can see I've put some effort into it – bath, perfume, lace undies, the lot. And if you were chivalrous you'd leave it at that, and only put up a token resistance. I know

I'm part of a case by day, but I'm something else again at eleven p.m.'

'How did you come by my address?'

'My dear Watson. It's in the phone-book.'

'What made you look for it in the phone-book?'

'Your eyes and hands. Say your hands.'

'Before or after you'd talked to Fazakerly?'

'Ah,' she said. 'This is bigger than both of us. But have it your way if you like. It was after I'd had my talk with Siggy.'

'And what did he talk about.'

'He said you were wonderful. He said you were a devil, but you were wonderful. And I agreed with him, of course, because that was exactly my impression. And I got to wondering where you lived and how and with whom you spent your evenings, and well, one thing led to another, and there were your hands, and here I am.'

'Did Fazakerly threaten you in any way?'

'He told me your name was George and that you were a bachelor.'

'Because he'd guessed you'd told his wife about Miss Johnson?'

'Yes, George, he'd guessed. No George, he didn't threaten me.'

'So it was you who told her?'

She gave another twirl. 'Don't you realize,' she said, 'what your manner does to me? You're so damnably tough and undentable, it simply turns me to a jelly. I said he'd guessed.'

'He'd guessed right.'

'I may have told her. Does it matter?'

'It matters when.'

'Say on Friday.'

'Not on Friday.'

'You choose the day.'

She swept odorously past Gently to the hard-seated settle, which was the summit of the comfort the den had to offer. She arranged the cushions fastidiously and spread herself at full-length. Then she opened a small vanity bag and lit a cigarette.

'Very well,' she said. 'Then we'll be serious. We'll play it your way, like tough hombres. It will give Mrs Jarvis time to settle in and I love it anyway, that's what's killing me. So give me the action, George. Chew me up and spit me out over your shoulder.'

Gently put a light to the bent pipe. 'I think you told me some lies,' he said.

'Oh, those hands!' Brenda Merryn moaned. 'I told you lies by the dozen.'

'Why?'

'A woman has to lie. Lying is fundamental with women. Especially to policemen with hands like yours. We just open our mouths and babble anything.'

'For example, you know a great deal about Beryl Rogers.'

'Not a great deal. Say more than I told you.'

'You know where she is.'

'Just look at my knees. Please. Once. I'll tell you anything.'

'Where is she?'

'She went to New Zealand.'

'But where is she now?'

'Does it matter? You must have enough on Siggy by now. You'll be picking him up again tomorrow.'

'I need to know where she is, Miss Merryn.'

'Not Miss Merryn, George. I can't stand it.'

'I think you can tell me.'

'You wouldn't look at my knees, and anyway Beryl Rogers didn't murder Clytie.' She made a gesture of dragging at the cigarette, and another gesture of exhaling the smoke. 'She's just a ghost,' she said, 'that's all Beryl is. A nasty, silly little, shallow little ghost. If you know the story you know what she is. I don't blame Clytie for what she did to her.'

'Have you seen her lately?'

'If you'll thaw I'll say yes.'

'In London?'

'Perhaps. I'm a terrible liar.'

'Within the last week?'

'Yes. I can't refuse you anything. Or if I didn't see Beryl, I saw someone just like her.'

'Where did you see her?'

'Must we talk of other women? It isn't worth your while, you know. Beryl Rogers is quite unnecessary. Suppose the ghost did walk a little and then vanished again at cockcrow. It was all an accident. You don't need her. As I'm a liar, it wasn't sinister.'

'But Mrs Fazakerly had seen the ghost.'

'Perhaps she only thought she saw it. Perhaps it was all done by mirrors. Perhaps it was hearsay after all.'

'You mean, she was told.'

Brenda Merryn smiled at him. 'You aren't treating

me right,' she said. 'You've got the key to me in your hands and you just won't turn the lock. In your hands. That's *double entente.* Give it a turn and see what happens. Give it two turns, one for luck. I have such a simple combination.'

'What I ought to do is give you a spanking.'

Her smile widened. 'Score to me. And then I'd blubber on your manly shoulder and that's the last step up the stairs. But I'm giving you value, if you only knew it, and I'm letting you ask all the questions. Suppose you answer me one.'

'What's that?'

'Why did you let Siggy go?'

She blew a thin stream of smoke at him and stirred, as though acknowledging the settle's hardness. The black diamond pattern of her legs readjusted and went still again. She'd been wearing pointed spur-heel shoes but she'd quietly pushed them off her feet. She watched Gently with amused eyes. Gently smoked, didn't reply.

'You're a suspicious man, George,' she said. 'But I can read you like a book. This is what you're thinking. You're thinking, This promiscuous bitch has really come here about the money. Am I right?'

Gently shrugged. 'Doesn't it rather stand out?'

She laughed. 'Yes. And it's partly true. I don't want to kiss that money goodbye. Be reasonable, George, it's an awful lot, and I'm only a weak, erring mortal. You dangled that money under my nose and I was rude as hell to the patients this evening.'

'You'd better make it up with Fazakerly.'

'Suddenly, I don't want to make it up with him. I see he's blown the gaff about me. But I didn't expect any different.'

'Perhaps he wouldn't make it up with you.'

'Of course he wouldn't. I'm a lost trend. Miss Johnson has twisted him round her finger and just now, George dear, she's quite welcome. But marrying Siggy is marrying a murderer, and that's too exciting for a girl like me. Oh, I probably wouldn't wind him up like Clytie, but just the same, the thought would be there.'

'He may not have done it.'

'Oh quite. But that isn't your position, is it?'

'We haven't charged him.'

'Not yet. You're waiting for one more little piece of evidence.'

'And you can give it me?'

The diamonds moved. 'You'd be surprised what I could give you. If you'd only climb off that high horse for a minute and let your blood flow normally. Have you talked to Sarah Johnson?'

Gently nodded.

'How much did she tell you?'

'That she'd known Beryl Rogers.'

'Only that?'

'She told me the reason why Beryl Rogers went abroad.'

'My, my,' Brenda Merryn said. 'The slut has more enterprise than I gave her credit for.' She chuckled. 'Wouldn't you think, judging as a man, that butter wouldn't melt in her mouth?'

Gently said: 'When did you make her acquaintance?'

She smiled from under lowered lids. 'Maybe I get around,' she said. 'Rochester isn't far from London. Heaven knows it was worth seeing the bint who could bridle and saddle Siggy Fazakerly. I never could, I give her that. Just put it down to curiosity.'

She drew on the cigarette a few times, then looked around for a place to stub it. Gently took the massive glass ashtray from his desk and leaned forward to put it on the floor by her. She said quickly:

'Don't go. I don't want you to miss what I'm going to say.'

He remained leaning. She looked at him steadily. She said: 'Yes. I can clinch the Fazakerly case for you.'

'So?' he said.

She swayed her shoulders. 'Of course, I'm in it for the money,' she said. 'I deserve that money as much as Siggy. More. I perform a useful service. And I'm not going to take up a moral attitude to justify myself for shopping Siggy. He shouldn't have dropped me so bloody suddenly when he ran across the Johnson chit. No kidding, cards on the table. He killed his wife and I want the money.'

'Very impressive,' Gently said.

Her eyes swam up to him. 'You slay me,' she said. 'All that sarcasm, what's underneath it? But you love what I'm saying, and you'll love me too.'

'Just what are you saying?'

'I was there in the flat.'

'You?'

'I could be lying. Don't forget I'm a liar. But I don't have an alibi, remember? And it's only ten minutes walk to Carlyle Court. Yes, I was there. I'm your eyewitness. Perry Mason wins again.'

He paused, staring at her. 'Why?' he said. 'Why were you at the flat?'

'Oh, this and that.' She drew a knee up. 'Naturally, we'll need a cast-iron reason. Let's say, for instance, I was wild with Siggy for throwing me over the way he did, and that I went down to Rochester on Sunday and recognized the creature he was playing around with. Terribly plausible, don't you think? I'd met the Johnson at the time of the trouble. So there I'd be with a beautiful card which I could hardly help playing. How do you like it?'

'Carry on,' Gently grunted.

'Praise enough,' Brenda Merryn said. 'So then I'd go round to the flat to play my card, which would be after lunch, after morning surgery. And I did go, and I did play it, and I just loved what it did to Clytie, and I knew that Siggy was due back so after I'd left Clytie I stuck around.'

'Stuck around where?'

'Do you remember the flat?'

Gently nodded.

'Then you'll remember the box-room. It's at the end of the landing and has a transom light, and I went in there and stood on a trunk.'

'And there you lit a cigarette . . . and waited.'

'Well,' she said, 'that doesn't need clairvoyance. And Siggy came in about ten minutes later, and Clytie hit him with all she'd got. For quarter of an hour, or thereabouts. I had the door ajar, listening. This was the pay-off, don't forget, and I was lapping it up like cream. But then it started to go wrong. Siggy was getting violent too. Suddenly Clytie began screaming "No, Siggy!" and there was a sound of a struggle and a shriek and a thump. How am I doing?'

'Keep right on talking.'

'Well, then Siggy bolted out of the door. He rang for the lift but it was in use, so he swore and ran down the stairs.'

'What was he carrying?'

'Carrying?' She hesitated. 'I don't remember him carrying anything. But if you say he was, that's dinkum with me. Only between ourselves, I didn't see it.'

'Then?'

'Then I went in and found her.'

'Where?'

'In the lounge. That's where the row was.'

'Where in the lounge?'

'Ah. I'm not too certain. Subject to correction, I'd say the floor. Yes, she was lying on the floor, with Siggy's belaying-pin beside her.'

'Did you touch the belaying-pin?'

'Not likely. After so much indoctrination by T.V. I didn't touch anything, especially Clytie. The way she was bashed didn't call for inspection. No, I spent a minute figuring my position and then I decided to follow Siggy. If I stayed and got myself mixed up in it I'd have some crude explaining to do.'

'You touched nothing, took nothing?'

'I'm wide open to suggestions.'

'How did you leave the building?'

'Inconspicuously. Down the stairs and through the mews.'

'Through the yard where the dustbins are kept?'

'Through the yard and straight ahead. But Siggy would have gone out through the front – he had his car there, remember. Then I went home, still inconspicuously. I honestly thought Siggy hadn't a chance. And it's a fact that I'm only here now because you didn't have enough on him to hold him.'

She smiled beautifully at Gently, lifting her face towards his. Her knee lifted and sagged, then lifted again and sagged again.

'And,' she said, 'you believe me, don't you?'

Gently gave a shake of his head.

'Yes, say you do,' she said. 'Flatter me.'

He looked at her, said nothing.

'At least,' she said, 'you don't know, can't be certain, whether I'm telling the truth or not. All the truth. Some of it. Most of it, bridged by intelligent guessing. You don't know, and you don't have to. That's for the jury to decide.'

'Your account doesn't square with Mrs Bannister's.'

She pouted. 'It can't be very different! Not if La Bannister told you the truth, though I daresay that isn't a blank certainty. But I'm not greedy. If it makes it easier, I'll square my details with hers.'

'And you think I'm going to accept that?'

'Of course. What do you have to lose?'

'By offering a perjured witness?'

'You don't know I'm perjured. And it will put Siggy

where he belongs. I suppose you're not going to tell me he didn't do it?'

'I'm going to tell you you didn't go back into the flat. And there was no struggle and no screaming. All the frills are imaginary.'

Brenda Merryn sighed. 'You're hard,' she said. 'And you're not being very intelligent, George. This isn't slipping halfbricks into somebody's pocket, it's really assisting the course of justice. You'll get the murderer, I'll get the money. Even Siggy can't grumble. And when it's all over George, wouldn't you rather have a rich mistress in Kensington than a poor one? Or since you're a bachelor, let's go further – say a rich Mrs George?'

'You'd go to that length?' Gently said.

She looked at him intently. 'Not for the money. But yes, I'd certainly go to that length. Because you don't quite hate me, do you?'

'In fact . . . you're offering me a cut?'

'Perhaps I am. Money is important.'

'I'm sorry, Miss Merryn. It isn't on.'

'You're still not calling me Brenda,' she said.

She lay back on the settle, her face gaunt in the dimmed light, one arm hanging over the settle-back, a hand trailing on the floor.

'Think about it,' she said. 'I'm levelling with you. You're not a kid for me to fool. You're not a hypocrite with froth on you. You're a realist, like me. And what I'm offering is real enough though it doesn't add up to soap-powder ethics.'

Gently rose. She looked up at him.

'Well,' she said. 'Are you tossing me out?'

'Have you transport?'

'I'd like to say I haven't. But that's my 1100 by the gate.'

'I suppose you can guess the advice I'll give you.'

She smiled ruefully at her lofted knee. 'I'm to go to Inspector Reynolds and give him a statement, and this time keep the screams and bodies out of it. Do you think I'll do that?'

'I think you'd better. It isn't just a question of the money, you know. You're placing yourself squarely at the scene of the killing at the right time. And with motive.'

Now she laughed. 'But you don't suspect me.'

'Also you've offered bribes to a police officer.'

'Not bribes and not to a police officer. Just myself. To you.'

They were silent a moment, then she said quietly:

'This is the queerest sort of thing, George. But I'm sincere, and you ought to believe it. Try to believe it. Even though I'm a liar. And now to surprise you I'll go quietly. Only help me on with my coat.'

She got up from the settle and he held the coat for her. When it was on she turned to face him. But all she did was give a little shrug and a long look. Then she went.

He heard the drone of the 1100 and its gears pass away down Elphinstone Road, then he took up the phone and dialled a number with raking strokes.

'Chief Superintendent Gently.'

'Hullo Chiefie. What can we do for you tonight?'

'I want information about Fletcher Bannister. Was a big man in plastics.'

'You name it, we have it. What do you want to know about him?'

'How he died.'

'Put your feet up. I'll have the details in half a minute.'

In half a minute exactly the man in the *Express* morgue was picking up his phone again.

'Fletcher Bannister, Chiefie. Killed in a car smash, October ten, fifty-nine. Was driving alone on the A4 at two-thirty a.m. Came off the road at Cherhill and hit a tree head-on. Estimated speed eighty-ninety. Bannister killed instantly.'

'Have you the inquest report?'

'This is it. Accident was witnessed by a truck-driver. Gave his opinion the crash was deliberate. No evidence of any contributory factor. Wife Sybil Bannister testified her husband's state of mind was normal, did not know he had taken the car out, knew of no business he might be attending to. Bannister wearing pyjamas, dressing-gown, slippers when found. Verdict, took own life while balance of mind was disturbed. Is it what you want, Chiefie?'

Gently grunted. 'Any mention of house-guests?'

'Not down here. Is there something we can print?'

'Not if you don't want a libel suit wrapped round you.'

He hung up and glanced at his watch. It was after eleven-thirty. He went down to the kitchen. There, as he'd expected, Mrs Jarvis was still sitting. As he entered she came out of a doze.

'Oh, Mr Gently! You'll be after your nightcap.'

Immediately she was bustling with milk in a saucepan and spooning rum into a beaker.

But she was giving him one or two sharp glances.

'Mr Gently,' she said. 'Was that – person – a client?'

And Gently lied slyly: 'She's one of our officers. She's doing decoy work round the Gardens.'

CHAPTER NINE

IN THE MORNING, resolving he might as well be hung for a sheep, he rang the office and left a message with Dutt and then drove direct to Chelsea H.Q. Reynolds had not yet come in, but Buttifant sat heavy-eyed in the C.I.D. room. He had a cigarette stuck to his lip and a piled ashtray at his elbow. He ducked his head and rose wearily. Gently motioned him to sit again. On the table in front of him was a scribbling pad and some pencilled-over sheets.

'Is that about the Rogers woman?' Gently asked.

'Yes sir. As far as we've got with her.'

'How far is that?'

'Well, we've traced her back here, sir. But nothing after she stepped off the boat.'

'But she is back here?'

'Yes sir. Landed in May of last year. I'm waiting to make some inquiries at the magazine offices, but their staffs don't seem to get in very early.'

'*Compact* influence,' Gently said. 'Where did you pick up with the Rogers?'

'At United Press sir, when she was working for them. They remembered about her and why she was sacked. Then we've traced her sailing on the *Rangitane* and coming back last May on the *Orontes*. But Worcester haven't found her family for us, and nobody we've talked to yet has seen her.'

'You wouldn't have a photograph of her, of course.'

Buttifant shook his head. 'We may have one coming. United Press run a staff magazine, and they're going to search their files for us.'

So Beryl Rogers was in the running; in the flesh, not merely as a ghost. Unless she had taken herself off again to some other distant part of the Commonwealth. She had returned, the necklace had been stolen and Clytie Fazakerly had died: if it were coincidence it was coincidence that needed a meticulous examination. And until then, in any event, Johnny Fazakerly was safe from a charge.

'Keep with it, Sergeant.'

Buttifant nodded dully and began rolling a fresh cigarette. Gently went out again, flicking a rubber plant, and sending a dry tab-end rattling to the parquet.

He drove to Vincent Street and parked the Sceptre as near as he could get to the Coq d'Or. The Coq d'Or was an opulent hotel with a 'family' tag and was popular with a certain class of visiting American. A commissionaire smiled at him in the foyer and a young waiter smiled at him in the reception hall and behind the desk were two other young men who smiled attentively when he approached.

'You have a John Fazakerly staying here?'

Yes; they didn't need to consult the register.

'Is he expecting you, sir?'

'I should think it likely.'

They smiled at Gently and at each other.

'If you'll follow me sir, please.'

One of them came out, beating the other to it by a head, and led Gently into a large, plush but empty lounge and set a leather-upholstered chair for him.

'What was the name sir? I'll find Mr Fazakerly for you.'

He darted out again, still smiling. Five minutes later he returned beaming to usher Fazakerly across the carpet. Fazakerly himself was not beaming. He stood looking at Gently till the young man left. Then he shrugged, threw himself into a chair and slowly held out his wrists.

'So it's a fair cop,' he said. 'I should have put Smith in the register.'

'Did you think we wouldn't keep tabs on you?' Gently said.

'I didn't think. That's my trouble. You wanted to see what I'd do, was that it?'

'No. Your being released was quite genuine.'

'Then why are you pinching me again the next moment?'

'This isn't a pinch. Just a morning visit.'

Fazakerly let his wrists fall again. He was perhaps still a little behind on his sleep. Some shadow remained about his eyes and his face was drained and colourless.

'Just a morning visit,' he said. 'Like that you still don't have me fixed up. I'm nearly inside but not quite,

I'm dangling around on a piece of string. Oh, it's great to be alive. I love a visit from the Chief Inquisitor.'

'This is better than a cell,' Gently said.

'You mean the smiling faces,' Fazakerly said. 'And how would you know about a cell anyway, when you're always on the outside looking in? No, it isn't better than a cell. I slept in that cell. I really slept. I didn't have to worry, I could relax, it was all over, I could sleep. Then you let me out and it started again, everything crowding in on me. You didn't free me. You set me adrift. I'm not even the bum I started out as.'

'Perhaps you never were that bum,' Gently said.

'Maybe I was, maybe not. But one thing's certain. In that cell I knew who I was, where I was. And since I came out my mind's been spinning. It's like a crazy machine I can't stop. It thinks and thinks, and I have to go with it. And I hate it. I hate what it keeps turning over.'

'What does it keep turning over?'

'It keeps turning over who killed her. Who must have killed her, if I didn't. And I'm pretty certain it wasn't me.'

'Only pretty certain?'

'That's my state. Facts aren't facts with me any more. It's like the world has gone back into the melting pot and facts are just what people believe. Maybe that's always the way with facts and we're kidding ourselves when we think they're different. I don't know. I don't think I killed her. I was certain yesterday. Not today.'

'Then who must have killed her?'

'It'll sound too silly. You have to start out knowing it wasn't me. That's to say you have to believe it, you have to worship it, make a fact of it, inspire the world to believe it with you. So that it's true for five minutes.'

'And when you've settled the metaphysic?'

'Then it all turns ugly. You've got a vacuum that sucks in belief and creates a fact you don't want.'

'Connected with your sister-in-law?'

Fazakerly nodded. 'Brenda told her. I'm sure of that. And I'm sure she was there when we were rowing.' He closed his eyes. 'I'm sure of too much.'

'You went to see her last night. Why was that?'

'Ask yourself, where would you expect me to go? She's the only relative I have in London, and I had to talk it over with someone.'

'What was her attitude?'

'That's the rub. She was sore as hell that I'd got out. Sore, shocked. It wasn't to plan. I could see it. She just wanted me back inside.'

'Did you row?'

'No. She's too intelligent to start rowing. But she was just like an east wind, and they blow through you and not round you. To make it natural she should have been happy for me, but she was too needled to bother with that. She believes like hell that you're going to get me. Not that I did it, that you're going to get me. She wants the money too darned much. She lets it show.'

'That's human enough. If she thinks you did it.'

'But I know I didn't, and I know she knows.'

'How?'

'She was there. Nobody else could have told Clytie.

And Clytie wouldn't have given it to me so raw unless she had an audience round the corner.'

Gently's head slanted. 'You're positive of that – it was the only reason for your wife's anger?'

'The more positive the more I think of it. In fact, I'd swear she was putting it on. It was out of character. She just didn't care. I was the fool to take her seriously. She had me spinning around like a blue-arsed fly and she didn't mean a bloody word of it.'

'Miss Johnson meant nothing special to her.'

'Sarah? Sarah was just a name.'

'That was the impression your wife gave you.'

'Of course. What could Clytie know about her?'

'That's what I'm asking you.'

'And I'm telling you. Clytie had never set eyes on Sarah. And if she had it would have made no difference, she was chums with half the women I slept around with.'

'So doesn't that indicate something special about Sarah?'

Fazakerly hesitated, his flecked eyes searching.

'Are you trying to tell me there is?' he said. 'Something you know about and I don't?'

Gently shrugged. 'How long have you known her?'

'Since last October. October the tenth.'

'Never before then?'

'No, never. Well, I may have seen her around once or twice.'

'You didn't see her around when she lived in Chelsea.'

'In Chelsea?' Fazakerly went still. 'She's never lived

this way, she belongs to Rochester. If she'd ever lived here she'd have told me.'

'What makes you so sure she belongs to Rochester?'

'Well . . . everything. Her parents live there.'

'You've met them?'

'No, but she talks about them.'

'And in a year you haven't met them. Isn't that strange?'

Fazakerly touched his forehead with his palm. 'I don't know,' he said. 'I'm going to pieces. Look, Sarah is the only thing I've got left. Just leave her with me. Don't play any tricks with her. She's my fact and I'm believing in her and I'm going to stay believing in her and you can't destroy her. Let her be!' He gave a moan. 'All right,' he said. 'What don't I know about her?'

'Only that she was a friend of Beryl Rogers.'

'Beryl Rogers?' He looked stupid for a moment. 'You mean that tart the trouble was about? Oh . . . now I see. Now I'm with it.'

'So your wife's anger may have been genuine.'

'Yes, genuine. Yes, I see.'

'She wasn't necessarily playing to a gallery.'

Fazakerly rubbed his forehead and groaned.

'Let me get it straight,' he said. 'Sarah didn't tell me. She didn't breathe a word of this. During all those times and intimacies when I told her everything, admitted everything. Yet she knew who I was. If it didn't mean anything it must have come out one time or another. That she knew Clytie. That she'd had a friend. That Clytie had fouled it up for her friend.'

'It's very natural she wouldn't tell you.'

'Natural. Yes. For a woman.'

'You might have suspected she wasn't genuine.'

'I might have suspected something else.'

'Then can you blame her?'

He hunched his shoulders. 'I don't know. It's how I said. All to pieces and in the pot. You look around and there's just nothing. So it's a small thing, very small, doesn't have any meaning. But the way I feel it's enough. It could be a bomb. It could be Gehenna.'

'When people talk like that they are usually excusing themselves in advance.'

Fazakerly looked at him bitterly. 'You're a pal,' he said. 'Job and you would have been real cobbers. But it's over with Sarah and me anyway, I knew it when I slammed the door on her. And now it's just laughable to think of reviving it. There's a thousand years gone by since then.'

'Did you ever really love her?'

'Yes. No. You tell me the answer. I built a framework of ideas and emotions round her and accepted the hypothesis of their validity. But I was conscious enough it was hypothetical and that my acceptance was not inevitable. And now that framework has detached itself and is floating away in the general flux. If you want ideas, those are ideas. But they don't mean anything. Unless you say so.'

'Perhaps you did suspect her in a vague way.'

'Perhaps I did. Who don't we suspect? In a perfect creation there's a sickness of egoism. We know that everyone is a little infected.'

'Did she ask much about your wife?'

'She may have led me on. I didn't need much asking.'

'Did she want to know how she spent her time. How she dressed. What jewellery she wore.'

Fazakerly hesitated. 'She did ask about jewellery – yes, she asked quite a lot about that.'

'About her favourite pieces and when she wore them. About that necklace she bought in Paris.'

'The necklace.' Fazakerly's eyes caught at him. 'Just where do you get your information?' he asked.

'In this instance from Miss Johnson herself.'

Fazakerly shrugged. 'Too simple, isn't it?' His eyes narrowed. 'Yes,' he said. 'She asked me a lot about the necklace. When Clytie wore it, where she kept it, whether and for how much it was insured. And I asked her if she was thinking of pinching it, and we had a giggle. Why do you ask?'

'Because it was pinched.'

'What? That necklace?'

Gently nodded. 'That same necklace. Your wife had it out on Monday morning, but by the time we arrived it was gone.'

Fazakerly sat up straight. 'But you're not suspecting Sarah! Good lord, I can vouch for her – she was at home all day.'

Gently shook his head. 'No,' he said. 'You can't vouch for her. And she was up here. She admits it.'

His light-brown eyes stared incredulously. 'You're having me on,' he said. 'You must be. I left her there getting down to some work and she was still there when I got back.'

'Still at her work?'

'Not at her work. She'd been down town to buy some bread—' He broke off. 'At least,' he said, 'I took it she had. She brought some bread with her when she came in.'

'So she wasn't in her apartment when you got there.'

'No. But she turned up ten minutes later.'

'In her car, of course.'

'Yes, in her car—' He got to his feet. 'This is madness!' he said.

Gently said: 'She came to London, because she admits it. She had a lunch appointment with one of her editors. And she didn't return straight away, she admits that, and she can't offer proof of where she went. But she had time to go to Chelsea and time to beat you back to Rochester. But if she didn't beat you back there it follows she may have left after you did.'

'Meaning?' he said.

'Meaning she could have been at the flat later than you.'

'And . . . pinched the necklace?'

'Perhaps,' Gently said. 'If nobody caught her in the act.'

He faced Gently agonizedly. 'No!' he cried. 'It's too utterly, bloodily preposterous. She couldn't have come back from doing such a thing and then behaved as she did with me. There must be something solid, somewhere. No woman on earth could have been such a hypocrite. It was genuine. If it wasn't genuine then chaos is come, and I'm a raving lunatic.'

'She didn't tell you where she'd been,' Gently said.

'I didn't give her a chance to tell me that. I was spilling over with injured egoism and wanting her to sacrifice to my degradation. And there was no question of Clytie being dead or any possible change in my situation. What we were arguing about was Clytie alive and me trying to find some honest work.'

'And she convinced you.'

'Yes. Yes. Nothing can be genuine if she wasn't, then. Good God, I've seen enough of women's games not to be taken in any longer. If you won't believe me on my own behalf, at least believe me on Sarah's.'

'She had a grudge against your wife,' Gently said. 'She seems to have shared in the Beryl Rogers disaster. That necklace was a sort of symbol, you know. Miss Johnson may have felt an irresistible urge to deprive your wife of it.'

'And all this while she was making me a tool?'

'She knew who you were when she picked up with you.'

'You can't make me believe it. There's no proof strong enough. Though she swore it herself, it wouldn't be true.'

'In part true. We have mixed motives.'

'Not even in part. I won't have that, either. If there's any connexion it's separate, coincidental. First she loved me, that's single and immaculate.'

'In the way you defined love?'

Fażakerly sank into the chair again. 'Why did I ever go to you?' he said. 'It must have been my evil star driving me along. The trouble is you're too damned understanding. I can't make any sort of front against you. You even stop me doing it with myself, you take the belief out of my words. So you want Sarah. Take Sarah. But Sarah isn't going to be any use to you.'

'Because,' Gently said.

'I'm confessing, damn you. It was me who killed Clytie and stole the necklace.'

There was a service bell on the wall near them and Gently reached over and rang the bell. A waiter came running through the swing doors as though his only duty was to answer that bell. He clicked his heels and smiled.

'What are you drinking?' Gently said.

Fazakerly glowered. 'Scotch,' he snapped.

'Export lager,' Gently said.

The waiter ducked and ran out again.

'This is one thing that money can buy,' Gently said. 'I can't afford to buy it myself, but I agree it's worth whatever you're paying for it. Just answer one question and I'll take you seriously.'

'I'm tired of answering questions,' Fazakerly said.

'What did you do with the necklace?'

'I slung it in the Medway.'

'Then I'm afraid you'll have to stay free and rich.'

The drinks came, a jar of Scotch with jumbo ice-cubes clattering in it, and a misty vase of lager. Fazakerly sat pat. Gently paid. Fazakerly drank slowly from amongst his bergs. His eyes were steady and distant. Just while he drank you would think he was dreaming of far atolls and sleepy guitars.

'So you're chopping Sarah.'

'I didn't say so.'

'That's the worst of you. You never say anything. You just apply pressures – that's your technique, isn't it? You harp away on one string till you drive a person gaga. And all the time you don't mean it. You're merely operating on their brain.'

'You think I don't mean it about Miss Johnson?'

'I think you've been laying it on too thick. She's a nice sharp tool for dealing with me. A bright lancet. The right-shaped blade.'

'I wanted your reactions. That's natural.'

'And now you've got them, what next?'

Gently grinned. 'I may even begin believing in your innocence.'

'That's crazy. Right when I've stopped believing in it myself.'

They drank some more.

'You said you'd never met Beryl Rogers,' Gently said.

Fazakerly nodded. 'I heard what happened though. Brenda filled me in on that. And it must have made an impression on Clytie because she always kept the memory fresh. That necklace was a symbol all right. It was pointing straight at La Bannister's heart.'

'Who would know your wife had it out on Monday?'

'Stockbridge of course. Perhaps Mother Lipton.'

'It was Mrs Lipton's day off.'

'She'd know that Clytie was going out.'

'Is she dishonest?'

Fazakerly shook his head. 'She's a damned old bitch,

but she's honest. We've had her ever since we moved there. She could've pinched a fortune if she'd wanted.'

'Who else would know?'

'La Bannister herself, and anyone who knew Clytie and knew she was going out. She always wore it. People would notice. If she'd booked a table, say, somebody might have done some guessing.'

'Did you know?'

'No. So I couldn't have told Sarah. And it's daft even beginning to suspect Sarah with La Bannister right on the spot. It couldn't have meant such a damn sight to Sarah, not enough to make her turn burglar. But it was vitriol to dear Sybil. The wonder would be she waited so long.'

'Tell me some more about your wife and Mrs Bannister.'

'More in what way.'

'About their relations.'

Fazakerly sipped.

'I've tried to believe that Sybil could do it,' he said. 'And I can't. Not quite. Though she may have done it, for all that.'

'Did she really love your wife?'

'Love-hate. That's the cliché. But all love is hate, you can't have one without the other. The trouble comes when you interfere with the natural balance of the phenomenon. Which is what Christ did. Which is why his results were so deplorable. Any creed that makes love a cult is on the straight road to Belsen.'

'And Mrs Bannister did that.'

'Yes. She made a cult of their relations. She had to,

it's her character. She's a curious strain of emotion and intellect. Clytie was a beast, but a natural beast, and in a strange sort of way you could sympathize with her. Perhaps that's why I stuck her so long and let myself drift into being a bum. But La Bannister is an unnatural beast. She's outside herself, pulling the strings. Her intellect won't let her emotions alone. She's an adulterated ego. So she wouldn't just love and hate like the grass growing but she'd try to separate one from the other and she'd set up love to be worshipped and in fact she loathed Clytie.'

'While at the same time being fascinated.'

'More than that. Parasitical.'

'She drew spiritual strength from your wife.'

'That's the key to the relation. You notice it with these split-types, they're drawn to more primitive kinds of ego. Perhaps Albert Schweitzer is such a one. What Hamlet needed was an aboriginal mistress. And Sybil found her primitive in Clytie. They'd known each other for years, you know.'

'And you can't believe Mrs Bannister would have killed her.'

'No. The other way round, I could believe that. Or somebody else, that I'd believe. But she'd always cringe before Clytie.'

'Someone else?'

'Say me for example. I daresay Sybil wouldn't stop at me.'

'Or say, a husband?'

Fazakerly took a long swig. He looked at Gently over the glass.

'Here we go,' he said. 'Dig, dig. You're always ahead of the game, aren't you? Dig and push. Dig and push. The art of being a top detective.'

'Inquest verdicts are no secret.'

'But knowing to look for them is a trick. What set you digging up Fletcher Bannister?'

'I like to know how people get rich.'

Fazakerly nodded. 'It's logical,' he said. 'That's what we murderers will never learn. But Fletcher Bannister did smash himself up, for all the wild women at the back of him.'

'You know about that?'

'I was there. October fifty-nine. Greystone Manor. Fletcher was a man and I was a mouse. He went out and got it over and I hung on and made squeaking noises. I'd been married just six weeks then. Him and me found out together.'

Gently drank. 'I thought it might have been that way.'

'It wasn't deliberate. Nothing of that sort. Clytie hadn't been seeing Sybil for a while and when they got together it hit the eye. Fletcher was one of these Podsnap busters who flinch if you happen to mention a choir-boy. He kept his head for a couple of days then flipped and broke into Sybil's bedroom. Not pretty. He took me with him. There was a stinking row which he didn't win. The next we heard him take off in his Mercedes and there was a lot of telephoning in the night.'

'How did Mrs Bannister take it?'

'She was scared more than sorry. But she needn't

have worried. Money talks. It washed out clean at the inquest.'

'And your wife?'

'She laughed.'

Fazakerly tipped his glass again. He looked at the ice left in the bottom, then set the glass on a table.

'Let me get in first this once,' he said. 'Creavey Merryn died of thrombosis. Creavey Merryn, her amorous uncle. He died in a nursing-home at Taunton.'

'Thank you,' Gently said. 'I did wonder about him.'

'You would, wouldn't you,' Fazakerly said. 'But you misjudged Clytie. She was a bitch without morals or scruples or mercy, but she wasn't a murderous bitch. In fact, there were moments when she could be affectionate. Of the pair of them, her and Sybil, Clytie was the one you could sometimes like.'

Gently shrugged. 'So they weren't murderesses.'

'No. Bitches, that's all.'

'Mrs Bannister and Miss Johnson you eliminate.'

'Sarah you can put right out of your mind.'

'Which brings us back to where we came in.'

Fazakerly nodded. 'It has to be that. If there's any sense in this mess at all, it must be Brenda who's at the bottom of it.'

'A planned killing.'

He went on nodding. 'Yes. Pinching the necklace would be a blind. What she's after is the money. She set me up: it's the only answer.'

'Unless of course . . .'

Fazakerly's hand twitched. 'Unless it was me all along?'

'That isn't what I was going to say.'

He paused. The waiter had returned and was smiling towards them.

CHAPTER TEN

THE WAITER STOPPED by Fazakerly and made his slight inclination.

'A Miss Junot would like to see you, sir,' he said. 'I didn't know if you were at liberty.'

Fazakerly looked at him wonderingly. 'I don't know a Miss Junot,' he said. 'What does she look like?'

'Very pretty sir. Young. I believe the lady is French.'

'Ah,' Fazakerly said. 'That explains it. It's Albertine. Send her in.'

The waiter went and Fazakerly grinned at Gently.

'Is she a friend of yours?' Gently asked.

'Depends on the emphasis,' Fazakerly said. 'I don't know the colour of her pyjamas. But yes, we're hail-bedfellow-well-met. I'm rather sorry for Albertine. And I'll tell you something: I think she was a disappointment to the ladies.'

'How does she know where you are?'

'Put it down to Gallic cunning. Though you could usually run me to earth here when I had any ready.'

Albertine entered. She beamed at Fazakerly, but

gave Gently some concerned little glances. She was wearing a black knitted dress which deftly moulded her curves and declivities. Her poppy-odour came before her and her blonde hair bobbed as she walked and her rouge was taken so high that her face appeared mostly cheeks. She was a strong, solid girl. One could easily imagine her among the milk-pails.

The waiter quickly set a chair for her and she sat down blushing and smiling.

'Well, Albertine,' Fazakerly said. 'What gives me the pleasure of a visit from you?'

Albertine didn't seem to find it easy to tell him. Her blue eyes rolled and smiled at him imploringly. At last she gave a charming pout and said:

'They do not tell me Monsieur is with you.'

'Oh,' Fazakerly said. 'Don't let that inhibit you. Monsieur is a friend. He's a sort of relative.'

'He is relative . . . ?'

'A cousin. You know about them?'

'Oh yes. A cousin. I know about cousins.'

'I thought you would do,' Fazakerly said. 'They're such a useful variety of relative. So what's it about?'

She looked languishingly at Gently. 'Oh well,' she shrugged, 'perhaps it does not matter. Perhaps it is good I am talking to Monsieur. Monsieur must know what I am going to tell you.'

'Yes, don't hide anything from Monsieur,' Fazakerly said. 'He has his methods, you take it from me.'

'His methods . . . ?'

'His way of breaking eggs.'

'Oh yes, I see. To make the omelet.'

She gave a gurgling little laugh, but didn't yet seem quite at her ease. She hugged a large handbag on her knees and moved her shoulders about awkwardly.

'It is my day off,' she said. 'You are told this. On every Monday is my day off.'

'That's why Monday is so dull,' Fazakerly said. 'I never run into her on a Monday.'

Gently said: 'What were you doing on Monday, Miss Junot?'

'I am doing – it is a friend I have, you understand?'

'Oh, we understand,' Fazakerly said. 'Don't write it out big for men like us.'

She threw him an indignant look. 'It is a friend – Giselle Lamereaux – she is from Chartres. She is in this country to learn your language. She is "au pair with Mr Jones".'

'With Mr Jones?' Gently said.

'No, not Mr Jones. That is a joke! There is no Mr Jones, he is not anyone, it is what one says. Is a joke.'

'Still, one rather envies him,' Fazakerly said.

'His real name is Meeson,' Albertine said. 'He is a big man, lots of money. Giselle is very happy. She likes your country.'

'And you spent the day with her?' Gently said.

'Oh yes. That is what I am going to tell you. And it is true, you may ask Giselle. Everything I tell you is true.'

'And they look you straight in the eye,' Fazakerly said.

'Oh!' she said. 'But it is you I am helping. Monsieur, pay no attention to this funny man. It is his way. He is a comical.'

'Where does your friend live, Miss Junot?'

'In Brewster Square, number twenty-nine. It is convenient. I can see her often. In the evening too, when I am not required.'

'And you were there all day?'

'Yes, since the morning. That is, we go out, but I am still with Giselle. That is, except for a little time in the afternoon. Giselle will tell you all this.'

'Go on, Miss Junot.'

'Then it is after lunch and we are going out to buy a skirt for Giselle. It is her birthday, this understand, and always we give each other presents. So I look in my bag and – no purse. I have left my purse in my room. I have two hand-bags, please notice, and it is in the other one I leave my purse. So I say to Giselle, Never mind, this will not take me one minute, and I go very fast back to the flat and fetch my purse from the other handbag. Then I return to Giselle, and we buy her a nice skirt at Peter Robinson.'

'What time did you go back?' Gently asked.

Albertine spread her hands. It is after lunch a little time. Perhaps it is nearly three o'clock.'

'Was your mistress there?'

'I did not see her, but yes, she will be lying down. I do not make any noise, this understand, in case I am detained by Madame. Madame is not an easy woman. There is perhaps some washing-up.'

'But you are sure she was there.'

'I think she is.'

'You heard her stirring, making sounds.'

Albertine pulled a face. 'No, no sounds. But I think she is, that is usual.'

'Did you hear any sounds from the flat above?'

'Oh no. One cannot hear from up there.'

'Movements, conversation?'

'Is not possible. No, I did not hear anything.'

'Did you see my car out front,' Fazakerly said. 'You know my car – the old Aston?'

She shook her head. 'I do not come in that way. It is not convenient, too far.'

'And this is all you have to tell me?'

'But no. It is only to tell you I was there. That is important, very important. You see Monsieur is very interested.'

She made an expressive movement with her shoulders and gave Monsieur a bright smile. Fazakerly was staring intently at her. His initial sparkle was fading.

'It is not anything I hear,' Albertine said. 'It is someone I see going up the stairs. Past the landing, up the stairs. And you know who? It is the sister.'

Gently said: 'Why haven't you come forward with this before, Miss Junot? You have a fairly shrewd idea that it's an important piece of evidence.'

Albertine twisted her shoulders and pouted. 'So?' she said. 'Do I know that? When Madame tells me it is certainly him, and you are everywhere looking for him? No, no, Monsieur, I do not think of it, the sister is often going up there. She will tell you herself if it is important. I do not think of it again.'

'You've thought of it now.'

'Ah, yes. Since you did not lock Mr Johnny up. Is not so certain then, is it? Perhaps he is not the one after everything.'

''So you go to him with this information.'

'Yes, Monsieur. To Mr Johnny. He is still in trouble, the funny man, and I like to help him. That is right.'

Fazakerly said: 'Thanks, Albertine. You're my only friend in London.'

Albertine made her face again and gestured with hand and shoulder.

'I see,' Gently said. 'So you saw Miss Merryn. Well, it comes in rather pat. You're sure it was her?'

'But certainly, Monsieur. I know the sister very well.'

'What was she wearing?'

Albertine hesitated. 'It is through the doors, this understand. One does not see it very clearly. Is not much light behind the doors.'

'Dress or costume?'

'I will not say! It is a dark colour, that is true. Yes, a dark colour . . . perhaps a costume. Perhaps the costume she wears to business.'

'Had she a hat?'

'Well . . . yes, a hat.'

'You saw her hat?'

'Yes. I think.'

'You think you saw it?'

'I will not be certain! I simply see her, a figure. So!'

'But you are certain that figure was Brenda Merryn.'

She spread both hands and yawed her shoulders. 'A

thousand times – I know that woman! I look, I see her, I say: Aha! Her clothes, her hat I don't notice. How do I know I should notice them? It may be Madame, that is what I am thinking, but is not Madame, is the sister. This is all that matters to me.'

'Don't bully the poor soul,' Fazakerly said. 'She's doing her best to give it to us straight. You've had nothing serious on Brenda till now. This is a break-through. It's the proof.'

Gently gave him a long stare. 'Yes,' he said. It's a break-through. But what it's proof of is another matter. I wouldn't take an oath on that.'

'You believe her, don't you?'

Gently said nothing.

'But for heaven's sake!' Fazakerly said. 'Why should Albertine come out with this unless she's telling us the truth? She can't be guessing about seeing Brenda. Brenda hasn't been mentioned up till now.'

'Oh, it is too bad!' Albertine wailed. 'I am telling the truth and he calls me a liar. And Madame will scold me all the same, because she wants it to be Mr Johnny. But you will see, Monsieur, oh you will see. It will come out. I am telling the truth. The sister was there, I cross my heart. May I fall down dead if it is a lie!'

'Here, take it easy,' Fazakerly said. 'Monsieur's trade is being suspicious.'

'But Mr Johnny, it is too bad – and all I wanted to do is help you!'

'You're doing all right, Albertine.'

'No – you see? He doesn't believe me. And why? I am foreign, a poor foreign girl, and that is the same thing as being a liar. Oh, too bad! I won't stop in this country. The money is nothing. I am going home.'

Gently said: 'Has Madame spoken of the sister?'

She stared at him furiously, breathing fast. 'I hate Madame,' she said. 'She is terrible. And I do not know that she was in the flat.'

'But has she mentioned Brenda Merryn to you?'

'She is a foul old woman, this understand. It cannot be spoken what things have gone on there, what she has done with Mrs Johnny and the others. I hate her. Tell her that! This is all too much, I will not stand it. I am a decent girl, I am brought up differently, I do not care how much she will pay me.'

'She has offered you money?'

'Always money. Money to let her play dirty tricks with me. At first, not money, I am to do it for nothing; but when I will not, then money. It is my name, you know that? Is the name of a girl in a stupid novel. Because I am named like this girl in a novel they think I will do dirty tricks like she did. Oh, oh. They were two pigs, if one killed the other it is no matter.'

'Are you accusing your mistress, Miss Junot?'

'Tell me this, Monsieur. Is it unlikely?'

'Have you reason to think so?'

'She is not in the flat. It is how you say, I would have heard sounds.'

'But it was not her you saw on the stairs.'

Albertine halted and looked sulky. 'No, it is true, that one is the sister.'

'You are still certain of that?'

'Oh yes. Certain.'

'Miss Junot, your mistress is a very rich woman. If she wanted something said she could pay someone to say it.'

Albertine stared a moment, then shook her head.

'She didn't approach you in this way?'

'Never. I would have spat on her money. I am not to be bought by such a woman.'

'She may have paid you to abuse her to us.'

'I do not need payment for that.'

'While still asserting you saw Miss Merryn.'

'If I had seen Madame, would I not tell you?'

'She has a point there,' Fazakerly said. 'I don't think she's kidding about hating Sybil. I think she'd love to implicate Sybil if she could make it stand up.'

'Oh!' Albertine cried, turning on him. 'You are as bad as he is, Mr Johnny. I am not lying. I have not taken money. It is true, all of it. So true.'

'Shsh,' Fazakerly said. 'Enough is enough. We're very grateful to you really, Albertine. You're the missing link, if you know what that is. Which is why Monsieur is putting you through it.'

'Monsieur is unfair. And it is you I come to.'

'You should have gone to Monsieur in the first place.'

'He does not like me. He is a great bear.'

'He's doing a job.'

'He is not a gentleman.'

Fazakerly shrugged humorously and tried to catch Gently's eye. Albertine pouted and stuck her chin out. But she too had a keen eye on Gently. Gently himself had no expression; he sat heavily, stooped in his chair;

his eyes were directed at his glass but it was doubtful if he saw it.

At last he said: 'Thank you, Miss Junot. You must go to the Police Station and make a statement.'

'Ah,' she said. 'Then you do believe me. It is all this time you are playing the fox.'

'We shall of course check your statement carefully.'

'And you will find it true.' She wriggled with fervour. 'I wish you to check it in every little part. This understand, Monsieur, I am truthful and decent.'

'Don't protest too much, old girl,' Fazakerly said.

'Oh, Mr Johnny!' she said, with a melting smile.

'Run along now, beautiful. We'll see more of each other.'

'It is to help you, Mr Johnny.'

'You're an angel.'

Albertine was suddenly coy again and she giggled and blushed as she rose to go. Her sophistication was an ornament that sat upon her very precariously. At the door she turned again to give Fazakerly an awkward wave.

'Well, well,' Fazakerly said grinning. 'I never knew Albertine cared. But of course, I'm a different character as of last night. This morning it's me who's wearing the cheque-book.' Then his grin faded. 'So that's it,' he said. 'I knew I had to be right, but I didn't think we would prove it. And I'm not sure now I wanted it proved. There was a time, once, when Brenda meant something to me.'

'Miss Junot has told us nothing fresh,' Gently said.

Fazakerly stared. 'You mean you knew about Brenda?'

'I saw her last night. She admitted calling on your wife. You are right. It was she who told your wife of Miss Johnson's connexion with Beryl Rogers.'

'She – admitted it?'

Gently nodded.

'And you didn't arrest her?'

He shook his head. 'It would be a curious thing for her to admit if in fact she were the murderer.'

'But . . . hell and all!' Fazakerly sat forward. 'Isn't that just the way you'd expect her to reason? That you wouldn't believe it if she came to you admitting she was the likeliest alternative suspect?'

Gently shook his head again. 'It isn't the way people work. They're rarely so devious when they're guilty of murder. If they're in the clear they try to stop there.'

'But perhaps she knew Albertine saw her.'

'If she knew that, would she have continued with her plan? In any case, her being there is no proof of her guilt; any more than your being there is proof of yours.'

'But I know I didn't do it!'

'That's an advantage you can't share.'

'But I do know. And Albertine is proof for me.'

'Perhaps Miss Merryn is arguing along the same lines. She knows she didn't do it, so she is certain that you did.'

'And you – you think that's the most likely?'

Gently shrugged. 'It's the more convincing. I mean from the point of view of a jury. It has the merit of simplicity.'

'Nothing will shake you. I'm guilty.'

'I didn't say that either.'

Fazakerly's hand went to his forehead. 'Oh God,' he said. 'The nightmare again!' He sat still for a few moments, the hand pressed to his head. Then he said huskily: 'Lock me up and take my shoe-laces away. I want an end, some sort of end. I can't stand dangling any longer. It doesn't matter whether I did it or not, just bring the chopper down and end the nightmare.'

'Where did you put the necklace?' Gently said.

'Don't torture me with that bloody necklace! Give me a hint of where you found it and I'll swear to heaven I put it there. Look, I've nothing to stay outside for. Even the money is damn-all. All that matters is a bit of certainty. Just help me: help me believe I did it.'

'Why don't you talk matters over with Miss Johnson.'

'She's dead. You killed her some while back.'

'You'll have to see her.'

'I don't like corpses. And we played our curtain on Monday.'

'I still think you should talk to her,' Gently said. 'She's on your side, it'll do you some good. What you want mostly is to talk your head off to someone as sure as you are you didn't do it. If you didn't do it.'

Fazakerly said weakly: 'How I love you.'

'And maybe she'll talk to you too,' Gently said, rising.

Fazakerly said nothing.

Gently went.

CHAPTER ELEVEN

SOMEBODY MUST HAVE noticed Gently's interest in the rubber plants because since his last encounter with them their leaves had been sponged and the fibre they grew in had been damped and raked. He paused a step to admire them then glanced casually at the desk; but the desk-sergeant was busily engaged in leafing through a bunch of forms. Gently fingered an immaculate leaf and left it imperceptibly nodding.

He found Reynolds with Buttifant in the office. They were both poring over a file of literature. They were so intent with whatever it was that they didn't notice Gently come in and both straightened up suddenly when he closed the door with a slight slam. Reynolds said:

'Chief, I think we're on to something!'

Gently nodded and pointed to the file. 'That'll be United Press's house magazine, will it?'

'Yes. It's just come in by messenger. I had Buttifant wait on purpose. I had a wild hunch, Chief, so wild I didn't like to mention it, but I think it's going to pay off. I think we've found Beryl Rogers.'

Gently smiled. It wasn't such a wild hunch. Do you have a recognizable picture?'

'You mean – you know?'

'I couldn't help guessing. Once I knew Miss Rogers had returned from New Zealand.'

Reynolds looked a little injured, but he made room for Gently at the table. The file was open at a page captioned: Fashion Parade's Staff Party. Opposite the letterpress was a half-plate photograph of men and women in evening dress but it was printed in coarse screen because the block had been borrowed from *The Holborn Advertiser*. Buttifant's yellowed forefinger pointed to a woman.

'That's her, sir. I'm ready to swear to it.'

Gently looked. 'That's perhaps Sarah Johnson. But she says she worked for United Press too.'

'But her name isn't here sir,' Buttifant pointed to the letterpress, at the foot of which was a list of names. 'There's twenty-four names and twenty-four people. Beryl Rogers is down here, but no Sarah Johnson.'

Gently peered again at the uncertain photograph. It had probably been taken by an amateur. The people in it had made an informal group and not all of them were within range of the flash. The woman in question was on the fringe of the group and only the plan-line of her face was shown effectively; but such as it was it suggested Sarah Johnson, and the slim figure beneath it was similar to hers.

'Check through some other entries. See if a Sarah Johnson occurs there.'

Reynolds said: 'But you've seen her, Chief. You recognize her don't you?'

'I think it's her. But if there was a Sarah Johnson we'd better know about it. That's a poor photograph, and house magazines are not noted for accurate reporting.'

'It's her all right,' Reynolds said confidently. 'It fits the facts too well for it not to be. All along we've wanted a reason for Mrs Fazakerly's being so angry and now we've got it. Someone tipped her off that her husband's girl-friend was Beryl Rogers. And this follows, Chief. Whoever tipped her was able to recognize Beryl Rogers. They'd have to know the old story and how much it meant to Mrs Fazakerly. If you eliminate Mrs Bannister, and I think you can do that safely, it leaves us with only one person – and Fazakerly fingered her for us.'

'Has Mrs Bannister's maid been here yet?'

'Albertine?' Reynolds shook his head.

'I've been talking to her. She'll make a statement. She saw Brenda Merryn going up to the flat.'

'She saw that!' Reynolds' eyes sparkled. 'That's a bit of luck for a good detective. I was wondering how we could tie her in, Chief. Now we've only to play our cards right.'

Gently got out his pipe and began to fill it. 'Go on.' he said. 'Let's have your version.'

'She did it, Chief. It fits everything. There's not a point it doesn't cover. Look at the set-up. She's the poor relation, and her step-sister's rolling in the family money; money that might and ought to have been hers, because it was her uncle who left it. What does she do? She seduces the husband, who may one day be left a widower; and that's how it stands until the husband drops her because he's become infatuated with another woman.'

'She might just simply have been in love with him,' Gently puffed.

'Do you really believe it was innocent, Chief?'

Gently shrugged. 'It's hard to tell. We'll carry on with your hypothesis.'

'She goes to look at this woman who's taking Fazakerly away from her, and she recognizes her as a woman who is obnoxious to Mrs Fazakerly. She can put the squeak in and get rid of her – Mrs Fazakerly was bound to blow her top – but she realizes it needn't stop there: she has a chance for the jackpot. There'll be a row. Fazakerly will clear out. If his wife's found dead, we're sure to suspect him. Then, if he's convicted, she collects the money by the rule of succession.'

Gently puffed some more. 'It sounds almost plausible,' he said. 'But.'

'Just wait a minute, Chief. I've been doing some thinking. This answers every one of your objections. Look, she knows when Fazakerly returns from Rochester and she times her visit just ahead of it. Then Fazakerly walks in when his wife is really worked up. Merryn goes off-stage to listen. She steps into the dressing-room next door. She sees the necklace, and it's safe to take it because Mrs Fazakerly is never going to miss it. So she slips it into her handbag and waits and listens till Fazakerly goes, then she rejoins Mrs

Fazakerly in the lounge and kills her while she sits talking on the settee. On the settee: you remember the point? It was likely to be someone known to Mrs Fazakerly. Not Fazakerly, because she was rowing with him, but someone she was talking to more calmly. Then Merryn leaves by the stairs and the back entrance, but she realizes how damning it would be if she were caught with the necklace, so she tips it into a dustbin. Then she has only to walk away.'

Gently puffed. 'It's neat,' he said.

'Chief, it covers all the facts. And now we've a witness to prove she was there. If we play it right we can nail her.'

'It's all you can prove. That she was there.'

'Let me have her. I'll make her talk.'

'If she doesn't talk you're no forwarder.'

Reynolds looked formidable. 'She will.'

Gently went on puffing. 'Before you go overboard! I hate to drag up Macpherson again, but the case you've just outlined will take some swallowing even if Brenda Merryn confesses.'

'But if it's true?'

Gently shrugged. 'I can't stop you. What I'm really saying is, keep in line. At best it will be a sticky case, so you'll do well to stay by the book.'

'I'll stay by the book,' Reynolds said. 'Don't worry, I've got the book weighed up.'

'Also, I think we should talk to Sarah Johnson. I think we should talk to her here.'

Reynolds grunted and stepped into the C.I.D. room and gave some orders to Detective Constable Baker;

then he returned to leaf through a directory and finally to dial a local number.

'Doctor Lithgow's surgery . . . Miss Merryn?'

He listened with a scowl growing on his face. His eyes, focused on an imaginary speaker, took on a truculent expression.

'How do you mean – have you been round there?'

The voice at the other end sounded indignant.

'Of course I have! Inspector Reynolds . . . all right, all right . . . you'll let me know.'

He hung up with a bang.

'She's missing,' he said. 'She hasn't been in to work. They sent someone round to check at her flat but she wasn't there. Nor was her car.' He looked at Gently. 'Do you think she's skipped?'

Gently said nothing for a moment. Then he got up, stuffing his pipe in his pocket.

'Come on,' he said. 'Let's get over there!'

Reynolds grabbed a patrol car and they drove fast to Knightsbridge Place. On the way Gently gave Reynolds a brief version of Brenda Merryn's visit to him. Reynolds asked one question:

'Was she upset when she left?'

But he asked it apologetically, and didn't seem to notice he got no answer.

They parked by the flats' entrance and went quickly up the steps. Gently rang. The bell tinkled briskly but there was no other sound from inside.

'What do we do?'

'Go in.'

Reynolds took out a thin bunch of skeleton keys. The third one slid back the bolt and the door swung open. They went in. The air was stagnant because of windows being closed but it held a scent which Gently remembered with sudden vividness: Blue Grass. They went through the lounge into the bedroom and into the bathroom and the kitchen. She was not there. The bed was unslept in. A tray with dirty crocks stood on the table. A big towel in the bathroom was still damp and stockings lay balled in a bedroom chair. The beaded slippers had been kicked off and left lying and the door of the wardrobe sagged open and a girdle lay spread on the bed. But Brenda Merryn was not there.

'Do you reckon she came back?'

'No.' Gently was searching through the wardrobe. Two padded hangers swung naked on the rail and the crimson dress and the coat were missing. Powder was spilled on the dressing-table and brush and comb lay thrown-down carelessly. A few blonde hairs were caught in the comb. On the label of a big scent-bottle a blue horse pranced. No: this was how she'd left it last night, after hastily dressing for his benefit. A severe navy two-piece, perhaps the one Albertine had mentioned, hung slightly bunched beside the two empty hangers.

'If she was away all night . . .'

'Her father lives in Bristol. You'd better ring him for a start.'

'Do you think it's likely, Chief?'

'It's possible. He's a solicitor, don't forget. Maybe she felt we were getting round to her, and her go at me was her last fling. It didn't come off, and she'd admitted too much. It was time to run to daddy.'

'You've talked to her most. There's nowhere else . . . ?'

Gently shook his head. 'That's all I know about her. If she isn't at home you'll have to issue a description. We'll take this photograph from the bedroom.'

They locked the door and went down again. They ran into their driver coming to meet them.

'Sir,' he said. 'This woman you're after – is she to do with the Carlyle Court job?'

'If she is, what about it?' Reynolds snapped.

'We've just had a buzz from control, sir. There's a woman out on a ledge at Carlyle Court and she's threatening to jump. I thought you should know.'

It was Brenda Merryn. They could see her plainly as soon as the car turned into Bland Street, a crimson smudge high up among the white cliffs and green-capped towers. A crowd was gathering. A T.V. camera van was already parked and being manned. At a dozen windows and balconies near where she clung people were clustered and cameras trained.

'She's outside the Bannister flat,' Reynolds muttered. 'My God, how'll we ever get her off there?'

'How would she have got out there?'

'Christ knows. There's a landing window, it must have been that.'

They roared up to the entrance and squealed to a stop. Stockbridge came running down the steps.

'She's going to jump!' he gabbled. 'I've been talking to her. She won't listen. You can't get to her.'

'How long has she been there?'

'Nobody knows. It was a tradesman down the street saw her. I rang the fire service and the police. But it's no good. You can't get at her.'

'Have you a rope?'

'That's no use. She says she'll jump if anyone goes near her.'

'Just get a rope and bring it up to us. And don't let any Pressmen into the building.'

Stockbridge's expression said it was too late, but Reynolds didn't wait to find out. Followed by Gently he jumped up the steps, ran through the hall and into the lift. The doors crashed shut and they glided upwards.

'First we'll talk to her,' Reynolds said. 'Mrs Bannister's veranda is on that level, we'll go out there and try talking her in.'

'And if she won't come?'

'We'll still keep talking to her. But I'll go up to the next floor with a rope. Then if the fire service can rig a net I'll take a chance of dropping a noose on her.'

'Not much of a chance.'

'I'm good with a rope. If she starts to sway I'll have her.'

They came out on the sixth floor landing. The first person they saw was Albertine. She was wailing and sobbing, and when she saw Gently she ran to him wildly and seized his arm.

'Monsieur – Monsieur! Oh, please, please . . . !'

'Out of the way, Albertine.'

'It isn't my fault, no, no. Oh get her in. Get her in!'

He shook her off, but she stuck at his elbow as they hurried through into the flat.

'Monsieur – Monsieur!'

'Be quiet, Albertine.'

'It isn't my fault. Oh get her in!'

At the door of the lounge stood Sybil Bannister with an expression of distaste on her fine features.

'I shouldn't be in too much of a hurry,' she said cuttingly. 'The sight of a policeman out there will probably do it.'

'Have you talked to her, Mrs Bannister?' Reynolds asked.

'Oh yes. I've talked to her once or twice.'

How long has she been there?'

'Since breakfast, I'd say. She's certainly been there a couple of hours.'

'A couple of hours!' Reynolds' grey eyes crucified her. 'And nobody's done anything until now?'

'It's a free country, Inspector,' she said mockingly. 'Unbalanced people may stand on ledges. Besides, does it matter? That is not my impression. I imagine Miss Merryn knows what she is doing.'

'And you'd just let her jump?' Reynolds said.

'Why not? It will save the taxpayers money.'

He brushed past her into the lounge. She looked at Gently.

'Crude,' she said.

Albertine was still moaning 'Monsieur . . . Monsieur,' and hanging to Gently like a ghost.

'You stay here, Albertine,' Gently said.

'Monsieur, it is not my fault, it is not what I said!'

'Of course it is, you stupid goose,' Sybil Bannister flung at her. 'That's exactly what it is. Your silly tongue drove her to it.'

'No, Madame, no, no!'

'Oh yes. But for you she would have got away with it.'

'Madame, no. I know nothing of that. I tell them only she is there.'

'And that's enough, you poor idiot. She's going to jump, and you're responsible.'

'Oh, no, no!'

'Go on the veranda. You may as well see her hit the pavement.'

Albertine gave a whimpering cry. Gently caught her round the shoulders.

'And you, Mrs Bannister,' he said. 'Won't you be coming on the veranda?'

'Oh no. I'm squeamish, Superintendent.'

'I wouldn't have thought it likely. With your experience.'

Her eyes slitted. 'With my what?'

'Wouldn't you have identified your husband's body?'

Her breath came hissingly and she stared hate at him. But she made no reply.

'All right, Albertine,' Gently said. 'You're not responsible for anything. Miss Merryn didn't know what you'd told us. That isn't the reason why she's out there.'

'Monsieur, oh please do something for her!'

'We'll do everything we can.'

'Let me help!'

'You stay here. Let nobody else into the flat.'

He went through and on to the veranda. From there Brenda Merryn's position was very plain. She was standing with closed eyes and with hands pressed to the cement facing on an ornamental tiled cornice set at the level of the veranda. Except for a narrow window some yards distant a blank wall stretched all around her. There was nothing to grasp. The first sway would send her plunging seventy feet.

She stood quite still, her head drawn back. She might have been basking in the watery sun. Her make-up was smeared around the mouth and had a soiled, stale greyness. Her face had no expression and no tension so that she could have been asleep. One of the diamond-pattern stockings had a ladder. On her forehead was a mist of sweat.

Below, after a recession of angled projections, green dormer-caps and the porch cornice, lay the neat squared pavement which fronted the entrance to the block. It was bare. The staring crowd had left a wide semicircle at that point. Nearest to it was the T.V. van and its big upward-pointing eye. And outwards stretched the slate roofscapes on either side of the quiet street to the embankment and the Thames and the trafficked span of the Albert Bridge.

'What for the love of Christ can one say,' Reynolds whispered without turning his head. 'That hag inside is probably right. When Merryn sees us, she'll jump.'

'What about your rope trick.'

'It's not on. See how she's pressed against the wall.'

'We should have a man on that window.'

'Two more cars have come. I'll phone down.'

He slipped away on tiptoe, though in fact there was a steady murmur of sound from below, and one could hear, from the direction of Millbank, the approaching clamour of a fire-engine. More heads were staring up from the dormers and cameras were held out and clicked. An attic window opened in the nearest building and a telephoto lens was trained through it. Gently looked at Brenda Merryn. Nothing seemed to disturb her. She remained in her trance of stillness, her hands spread on the rough facing.

'Miss Merryn,' he said.

'Go away, George.'

Her immediate response was uncanny. It was as though she'd known very well he was close to her and had been anticipating he would speak. Yet her eyes were closed.

'Miss Merryn,' he said. 'Where have you been since you left me last night?'

'Around and about,' she said. 'Mostly around. But about too. Around and about.'

'Why didn't you go home?'

'Don't ask silly questions. They sound so pathetic from where I'm standing. I'd nobody to go home to, so I didn't go home. It's the way it gets you. Silly answer.'

'Did you just drive about London?'

'Yes, London and other places. Like Paris and New York. Or it might have been Rochester.'

'What were you doing there?'

'Say I was looking for a sailor. Go away George. And tell them if they put their bloody ladder up, I'll do it.'

Reynolds came tiptoeing back.

'Is she talking to you?' he whispered.

'Send a message down to that fire-engine. She says she'll jump if they use the ladder.'

Reynolds swore under his breath. 'They have to make that stupid din,' he said. 'If they'd come quietly they might have nabbed her.'

Gently shook his head. 'I think she's watching.'

Reynolds said. 'I've manned the window. We just beat a press-photographer to it. And I'm having them send us a couple of policewomen and a constable who spends his leave rock-climbing. I want to talk to those firemen. I think we could rig something on the roof. If we could drop a man in safety-harness he might grab her before she goes.'

'She'll go. If she wants to.'

'Talk to her, Chief. You may win.'

Reynolds glided away again. Gently went on watching Brenda Merryn. She hadn't moved or flickered an eyelid while he and Reynolds had whispered together. But now she said casually:

'I don't like Reynolds. I think it's his moustache, it's too damn British. And he's, what shall I say, too full of his own efficiency. He'll never be a big man like you.'

'Are you feeling big?' Gently said.

'Tired,' she said. 'Tired, George. And it's nice just to stand here with the sun warming me and knowing all my problems are solved. I feel so happy and content.

I needn't open my eyes again. Don't let anyone come interfering with me. I don't even want a cigarette.'

'Your father will have to know, of course.'

'Daddy. He's very understanding. He wouldn't want me to stay on here if there was nothing for me to stay on for. I've written him a little letter, you know. It's in the glove-compartment of my car.'

'Why did you come to me last night?'

'I wanted to. That's all.'

'Why?'

'There isn't any why. It was suddenly with me. Women are like that. Oh, I wanted some other things too, like Uncle Creavey's thousands, and getting even with Siggy. But they were just by the way.'

'Condemning your brother-in-law was by the way?'

'Getting even with him was what I said, George. I don't condemn him. I'm not a Christian. But I wasn't going to let him get away with it. You see, I didn't altogether hate Clytie and I think she had moments of liking me. We weren't quite sisters so we weren't quite enemies. In a sense you could call us friendly neutrals. But I don't think you're going to understand that, are you, because I did for myself, coming to you. I made a mistake, George, I thought you'd be with me. Damn silly. I always lose.'

'In fact, you offered me bribes and false witness.'

'Both. But that wasn't my mistake.'

'What sort of an impression could you have hoped to make?'

'It depended so much on you, didn't it?'

Her lips quivered, and he could see her fingers

pushing harder against the cement. Below, a man was stationed on an expanding ladder, but Reynolds was also there talking to the crewmen.

'I knew I'd lost, George. When I drove away. When I waited at the lights at Finchley Road. It was a big throw, all or nothing, and it didn't come off: you slapped me down. Because you had to believe that Siggy had done it. Or you had to want me enough so it didn't matter. And it wasn't the one way or the other. I was just left driving away in the night.'

'There's still time to give me a straight statement.'

Her head moved almost imperceptibly. 'No. Too late. I told you too much in the wrong sort of way. Because you think Siggy is innocent. That was my mistake.'

'It doesn't follow you are guilty.'

'Not while I'm standing here, does it? Don't bother, George. I can imagine the things one usually tries on these occasions. Keep patient talking. Talk is therapeutic. Talk helps to resolve the depressive tendency. Suggest optimistic views. Offer food. But keep patient talking on any subject.' She paused. 'I'm sorry,' she said. 'Perhaps you do care a little about me, George. But it can never be much, not after last night, so don't bother kidding me. I'm sunk.'

'I can only repeat what I said, Miss Merryn. Other people are involved besides yourself.'

'But I offered bribes and false witness, didn't I? And I was there. Now you can prove it.'

'I can prove it?'

Her lips twisted. 'La Bannister saw me. I didn't

know that. I'm not sure La Bannister knows it either, but her false witness is doubtless better than mine.'

'Mrs Bannister told you this?'

'Hasn't she told you? Oh, but she will when you give her a chance. She was out on the veranda before you got here, giving me a few valedictory words. But notice I say that she's a liar. I'm pretty damn certain she didn't see me.'

'Did she say where she saw you?'

'Here, she said. She'll have details ready, by now.'

'When did she say this?'

'What does it matter. When she was last out here before you came.'

Gently was silent. Above the murmur of the crowd he could hear Reynolds' voice giving instructions. The man on the ladder was climbing down again though with apparent reluctance. Out of the van they were lugging equipment which included booms and a big pulley. Another police car was approaching. Two constables were moving about in the crowd.

'If they're planning something,' Brenda Merryn said, 'you'd better shout down and tell them to lay off. Tell them I appreciate their attention, of course. But the first rope I see, I'll be on my way.'

'Miss Merryn,' Gently said.

'Brenda, George.'

'Miss Merryn, I want you to listen carefully. I believe you have evidence of critical importance, and I need to have a statement from you.'

Her lips went wry again. 'Of critical importance to whom?'

'To us. To the investigation of this case.'

'But not to me.'

'To you too.'

Her head moved. 'Too late,' she said. 'I cared once. I don't now. If last night hadn't happened and you were asking me the truth I'd give it to you. But not now.'

'You don't care any longer who killed your step-sister?'

'I can ask her myself in twenty minutes. You'd better have a medium on tap. I'll try to pass back a message.'

'If it wasn't you—'

'I tell you I don't care.'

'Miss Merryn—'

'Go away, George,' she said. 'You won't call me Brenda, which is all that matters. I'm going to jump. Go away.'

Someone touched his shoulder. It was Reynolds. He was holding his finger to his lips.

'Shsh! They're on their way up, Chief. Keep her at it. It'll be O.K.'

Gently shook his head. 'She knows they're up to something.'

'The bloody bitch. We'll have to try it.'

'No. She'll jump.'

'What do we do then?'

'Put a net out. Hope.'

The fire-crew, augmented by a second brigade, assembled and manned a catching-net. Brenda Merryn didn't seem to notice the stretched grey canvas that bloomed below her. Perhaps she guessed what the fire-chief was saying: 'She'll be damned lucky not to go clean through it!' – or perhaps she imagined she could throw herself clear. From the veranda the net was not impressive.

Reynolds' two policewomen arrived. One was a plain-faced girl with huge hips. The other had a snub nose and freckles and a degree of brusque charm. Her name was Fairley. At her request she was left alone with Brenda Merryn. In the lounge one heard her voice, sympathetically homely, engaged in continuous monologue.

'She's pretty good,' Reynolds said to Gently. 'I'd as soon have Fairley there as anyone. What did Merryn talk about?'

Gently grunted and looked at Reynolds without seeming to see him.

Mrs Bannister had abandoned the lounge but Albertine sat sniffing in a corner. Every so often she jumped up and ran to poke her head through the french windows. Then she came back to sob afresh; and each time Reynolds frowned at her.

'I suppose she's no good to us?' he murmured.

'Albertine?'

She heard her name. In a moment she was beside them and tearfully clutching Gently's sleeve.

'Oh Monsieur . . . let me help!'

'What can you do, Albertine?'

'I can talk to her, Monsieur, I can plead with her. Oh please, please let me do this.'

Gently looked at Reynolds. 'How is Fairley doing?'

Reynolds shrugged. 'She's doing all right. But I can't hear her getting any results, and she's been at it now ten minutes.'

'Monsieur, please – please!' Albertine said.

'No harm in trying her,' Reynolds said.

Gently stared at Albertine for a space. Then he nodded. 'Right,' he said.

Policewoman Fairley was withdrawn and Albertine ran to take her place. Her first passionate appeals were so broken with sobbing that they were barely comprehensible. Policewoman Fairley had come in frowning, and for a while she listened carefully. Then she said to Reynolds:

'I'm not certain, sir, that Merryn isn't putting on an act.

'Doing what?' Reynolds gaped.

'You know I've had some experience, sir. And the way Merryn is behaving suggests to me she isn't serious.'

She gave Gently a little look.

'It's this way, sir,' she said. 'If they really mean it they want to talk to you about the rough deal they've had. They want people to know about that. They want to take it out of someone in pity. And Merryn just stands there smiling a bit and lapping up what you say to her.'

'But hell – look where she's standing!' Reynolds said.

'That doesn't mean very much, sir,' Fairley said. 'I know it would do for you or me, but some people have a head for heights. My boyfriend has. He'd go out there. And there are lots of window-cleaners who would.'

'You're saying she's doing all this for a kick?'

'I don't know why she's doing it, sir. I imagine she wants to impress someone. But I don't know all the circumstances.'

'She wants to impress someone,' Reynolds echoed. 'Well, she's doing a nice job with me.'

'And if she doesn't succeed in impressing them?' Gently said.

Fairley looked aslant. 'I don't think she'll jump.'

They were silent. Albertine was telling Brenda Merryn that she, Albertine, alone was to blame. The crowd below was making less noise, perhaps intrigued by Albertine's colourful oratory. Mademoiselle must come in, Albertine was saying. It was a big mistake. Monsieur knew. She would be sorry, that Mademoiselle, if anything happened she would be sorry.

Reynolds gave a grunt of disgust. 'So how's it going to end?' he demanded. 'Is she just going to have her fling, then walk in here with a beautiful smile?'

'Something like that, sir,' Fairley said. 'When she gets tired or hungry.'

'And we still have to make it a big production.'

'I'm afraid so, sir. In case she's serious.'

Gently raised his hand. 'Listen.'

Albertine had stopped talking and the crowd had gone quiet. All one could hear now was a scuffling sound and a series of frightened whines. Then there was a wail of terror from Albertine and suddenly Brenda Merryn's voice was shouting and a shuddering sigh came from the crowd and Albertine was screaming.

'You French imbecile,' they heard Brenda Merryn shouting, 'you haven't the head for it. Get back on the veranda!'

They ran out. Albertine was on the ledge and had already advanced some steps along it. But she was almost petrified by her situation and was screaming like a terrified animal. She was shrinking against the wall and scrabbling at it while gingerly moving her feet, and with every step she screamed piercingly and jerked in a perilous manner. Yet she didn't stop. By an act of will she was driving herself along the ledge. She couldn't prevent her fear bursting nakedly from her, but she never faltered in her intention.

'Some of you – grab her!' Brenda Merryn cried. 'Can't you see she's going to fall? She's got no head, she's stark raving. She'll have us both off if she gets here.'

'Back off to the window,' Gently called.

'Damn you, I won't. I'm here to stay.'

'If she has to turn she'll probably fall.'

'Then one of you big brave men come after her.'

'Mademoiselle,' Albertine screamed. 'Mademoiselle! Come in now. Oh come in now!'

She was trembling and wobbling at the knees. But still she kept going forward.

Brenda Merryn swore. She looked towards the window, from which the head of a constable projected, then at the screaming, shuffling figure, which seemed about to collapse at any second. Her lips compressed. She began to move, quite coolly, towards Albertine, her hands, one advanced, one trailing, sliding lightly over the facing. Within a yard of her she stopped.

'All right. This is far enough, Albertine.'

'Mademoiselle . . . you are coming in!'

'Yes. Stop there. Don't look down.'

'But you must come in!'

'Albertine. Do exactly as I say. Don't try to grab me and don't look down. Just look at me and rest a little.'

Then she smiled and kept smiling. And after a moment Albertine stopped screaming. The screams became a subdued wailing, like the keening of a child. Albertine clung with all her might, her nails edging at the cement, but she didn't scream, and her hysterical breathing began to grow more regular.

'Now Albertine, listen closely. You see I'm not frightened, Albertine?'

'Mademoiselle—'

'I'm not frightened because I don't keep looking down. I'm standing on a ledge and it's quite safe and I know it's safe and I don't think about it. In fact it's rather grand up here. There's a fine feeling of lots of space. Don't you feel it too?'

'Yes, Mademoiselle, but—'

'Now we're going back to the veranda. I'll tell you how. Look at the wall, then turn your feet. First the right foot, then the left.'

'I do not . . . cannot . . .'

'Look at the wall. Let your feet take care of themselves. Are you ready?'

'Mademoiselle.'

'Now. Right foot . . . left foot.'

And Albertine turned. Quite easily. She faced the veranda, her eyes rolling. She stood, mouth open, fingers clutching, waiting to hear the next instruction.

'Don't press with your hands, Albertine. Don't try to look at your feet. Look at Monsieur George on the veranda. Now shuffle along till you reach him.'

Albertine shuffled. In strict obedience she kept her eyes firmly on Gently, and though he wanted to glance over her shoulder at Brenda Merryn he dared not lose that fixed glare. She came on steadily. Her wild expression had a ghastly abstraction in it. She no longer trembled but seemed to function mechanically with her terrified mind at a distance.

'Say something to Albertine, George,' Brenda Merryn said.

'Albertine,' Gently said. 'We could all use a cup of coffee.'

'I know I could,' Brenda Merryn said. 'A cup of strong French coffee, Albertine. The way you make it, hot and strong. I'm longing for a cup of your coffee.'

'Is she good at coffee,' Gently said.

'You bet she is,' Brenda Merryn said. 'If you haven't tasted Albertine's coffee you don't know what coffee tastes like yet.'

'I'm looking forward to it Albertine,' Gently said. 'I've a sudden thirst for some good coffee.'

'She makes the best coffee in Chelsea,' Brenda Merryn said. 'And she'll rustle it up for you in five minutes.'

Albertine's face made a frantic smile to which the eyes did not contribute. Her head was tilting further and further back as though in an effort to prevent her eyes slipping downwards. The gap decreased. It was just at the end she nearly came to disaster. She reached for Gently's hand too soon, missed it and rocked for a second, fingers weaving.

'There,' Brenda Merryn said, 'there. You two will never be sweethearts.'

And Albertine made the last step and was hauled over the iron railings of the veranda.

She collapsed in the arms of a policewoman and was half-led, half-carried inside. Below, the silence of the crowd erupted strangely into a gust of roaring, clapping and cheering. Brenda Merryn remained short of the veranda. Her hazel eyes faced Gently's. She deliberately looked down at the scene beneath her, waved to the crowd, then looked back at Gently.

'So you do have a head for it,' Gently said.

Brenda Merryn's chin lifted and she made a rude noise.

'It's a useful gift.'

'Go to hell, George. And stand back from that railing. Or I'll go down the short way.'

She swung herself into the veranda and prepared to stride past him. He caught her wrist.

'Wait,' he said. 'If you go down there the press'll murder you. And I want you here.'

'You want me,' she said. 'That makes a change at all events. So I'd better stay.'

She snatched her wrist away and marched through the french windows.

Reynolds touched Gently's elbow. 'Chief, I'm in a daze,' he said. 'Ten minutes ago I'd have pinched Merryn. Now I'm foxed again. Give me a lead.'

Gently hunched. 'You can pick up Fazakerly for a start.'

'Fazakerly?'

'Have him brought here. And Sarah Johnson, when she arrives. I want them all. We're going upstairs. We're going to do some hard talking. We're going to show Sarah Johnson to Mrs Bannister. We're going to beat their heads together.'

'You think they'll unclam?'

'I think maybe. Something should come out in the wash.'

'Right Chief. I'll fix it.'

'And something else.'

'What?'

'That coffee.'

CHAPTER TWELVE

THE COFFEE WAS drunk and it was coffee which Albertine had insisted on making. She was surprising. Apparently a state of shock was no impediment to her. After sobbing and shaking and moaning and rather comically upbraiding Brenda Merryn she remembered the coffee and, without reference to Madame, went trembling to the kitchen to brew it. It was excellent, if not entirely the best coffee in Chelsea. Madame accepted a cup and drank it silently beside the Chippendale bureau-bookcase. Madame was saying very little. She watched the invaders with frigid eyes. She watched Albertine. Albertine went out of her way to avoid catching Madame's eye. And so the excellent coffee was drunk in a curious and uneasy atmosphere.

Reynolds had gone to fetch Fazakerly but he had left the two policewomen with Gently. They accompanied him and the other three women up the stairs to the Fazakerly flat. The flat felt chilly. Stockbridge, probably, had decided to cut off the central heating, and though thin October sun slanted into the lounge it had small effect on the temperature.

Mrs Bannister shivered. 'If we must come here I don't see why we should freeze to death. Can't we have some heat?'

'If you wish.'

'Albertine. Fetch a heater.'

Albertine hurried out and returned lugging a big Belling. She knew where the point was and carried the plug to it and the Belling glowed and creaked into life. Mrs Bannister took a chair and sat beside it, spreading her hands to the current of warm air. But she still seemed to feel the chill of the room and now and then gave another shiver.

Brenda Merryn had gone across to the settee. Her sharp eye noticed the stains. She glanced at Gently, who made no sign, and she gave a little shrug.

'Poor Clytie.'

Mrs Bannister said fiercely: 'I wish Miss Merryn would spare us her comments.'

'Come off it Sybil,' Brenda Merryn said. 'You'd better keep relaxed while you're up here. George hasn't brought us here for fun. He hopes this room is going to crack us. If you've any sense you'll act curious and have a look at the settee.'

'Thank you so much. But I'm not an actress. And perhaps you're not a good one either.'

'Miaow.'

'I can guess about the settee.'

'I couldn't. And I find it oddly suggestive.'

Mrs Bannister lifted her head. 'Is this woman

working with you?' she asked Gently. 'I find her offensive. I don't have to remain here and unless you put a curb on her I shall leave. I should have thought there was not much doubt of where she stood after her peculiar display this morning.'

'Touché,' Brenda Merryn said. 'First blood to me. And don't forget your own standing has its points of interest.'

'You are impertinent.'

'I can't help it. It's your pose, Sybil. One has to bait you.'

'Perhaps they will teach you different in Holloway.'

'Yes. To me it wouldn't come natural.'

The second policewoman smothered a giggle but unfortunately Mrs Bannister heard it. She sprang to her feet. She found Gently standing with his back to the door.

'Sit down, Sybil,' Brenda Merryn said. 'Doing the duchess isn't good enough. It takes more than a repertory job to impress George. Sit down and think up some new insults.'

'You coarse bitch.'

'You charming parasite.'

'You should be whipped.'

'You should know.'

'You are an envious and scheming and insolent person.'

'Dear Sybil. You'll shoot your bolt before we come to the big picture.'

Mrs Bannister swung round on Gently. 'Superintendent, I insist on leaving. You have no right to keep me here and if you try I will sue you. Stand aside.'

'You may go, Mrs Bannister.'

'I certainly may. Let me through.'

'But we shall have to fetch you again directly to identify a certain person for us.'

She halted, fronting him. 'Oh. Who?'

'I would sooner you told us that when you've seen the person.'

'This is very mysterious. I suppose it isn't an invention to keep me a prisoner in this room?'

Brenda Merryn chuckled. 'I doubt it, Sybil. I think I can guess who George is bringing here. George is sharp. You'd better prepare yourself. He's going to hit you, and it's going to hurt.'

Mrs Bannister threw her a scorching look. 'I repeat. Who is this person I am supposed to identify?'

'A person connected with the case, Mrs Bannister.'

'I wish to know more.'

'I believe I hear them arriving.'

There was a sound of the outer door being unlocked and Albertine rose as though to attend to it. Gently motioned her to sit again. Mrs Bannister stood undecided and staring suspiciously. There came a tap on the lounge door. Reynolds entered, followed by Fazakerly. Then Sarah Johnson.

When Mrs Bannister saw her she gave a gasping cry and slithered to the floor in a faint.

'You are Beryl Rogers?'

Sarah Johnson's flattish face was pale and tight. She walked into the room and slowly across to the window and stood looking out with her back to them. The policewomen were attending to Mrs Bannister, who they had carried to the settee. She was groaning to herself, her eyelids flickering, her hand fluttering about her bosom. As still as Sarah Johnson stood John Fazakerly. His wide eyes were on her back.

'Yes.'

'My God!'

Fazakerly jerked and his eyes seemed to fade. In a taut, brittle voice she continued:

'At least, I was until five years ago. Then I became Sarah Johnson. I've been Sarah Johnson ever since. It isn't my name on the record. But it's my name except to the family.'

'Only you were involved in that incident with Mrs Fazakerly.'

'Yes.'

'There was no friend as you described.'

'No. All invention.'

'And you hid your true identity from John Fazakerly, knowing who he was.'

Her head nodded.

'Can you add to that?'

'Yes.'

Brenda Merryn said: 'Don't be a fool. It's all right with me if you put your head in a noose, but there's no need to make it so easy for George.'

'You're the woman who talked to me on Sunday,' Sarah Johnson said, turning. 'Yes, you followed me into the toilets and asked me for a light. And now you're here. I'm beginning to see. Who are you – a policewoman in plain clothes?'

Fazakerly laughed harshly. 'That might be a description, but Brenda didn't make her report to the police.'

'Who is she, Johnny?'

'She's Clytie's step-sister.'

'Clytie's . . . oh.'

'Has the penny dropped?' He dug his hands savagely in his pockets. 'She had the advantage of me,' he said. 'She knew what Beryl Rogers looked like. I just knew she was a bint of Sybil's.'

'That's not fair, Johnny!'

'It's fair and it's true – and just about the sort of bum's luck I'd have. You were special. You were my one woman. For you I went overboard. Sybil's bint.'

'Oh, you're so unfair! I love you, Johnny.'

'You hated Clytie is more like it. I was some luck, a perfect innocent. I'd never have known but for Brenda.'

'I love you. Believe it.'

'I'd never have known. I'd have gone on living in my world of dreams. I'd have believed ever after I'd found the one exception among women, the one who saved all the rest, who redeemed the general rottenness. And Brenda's saved me from that anyway. There's no exception. Women are crap.'

'Thank you so much, Siggy,' Brenda Merryn said. 'I'd hate to leave you with romantic illusions.'

'All I care about now,' Fazakerly said, 'is who is responsible for this bloody mess. I thought it was Brenda till a moment ago and it fits Brenda best. But Sybil's bint would go after that necklace. And Sybil's bint was here on Monday.'

'Johnny, you can't think—'

'The necklace!' he jeered. 'The necklace you wanted to know so much about. It vanished on Monday, so I'm told, and I'm sure you'd think stealing it a fine revenge. But you should have hidden it or thrown it in the Thames. Because Monsieur has found it. And it probably has prints on it.'

'Does it have prints on it?' Brenda Merryn asked.

Gently met her glance stonily.

'Of course it does,' Fazakerly said. 'It'll have prints all over it. The prints of the thief. Of the killer.'

'Which would let you out, would it?' Brenda Merryn said. 'I ask purely for information.'

'Yes it would let me out.'

'Isn't that splendid. A pity everyone knows jewellery doesn't take finger-prints.'

Sarah Johnson said: 'Johnny, you're angry. This isn't really you speaking at all. You're accusing me of this because I deceived you and not because you believe I'm guilty. And it's terribly unfair. I've been trying to protect you. I love you sincerely whatever you think. I'm not the one who's to blame for all this, I'm the one who's suffering for it.'

'How she talks!' Fazakerly snarled. 'A woman's answer isn't far to seek. I was your cat's-paw, Sybil's bint: try to talk that off the record.'

'Johnny, I swear I was sincere!'

'Yes, in the manner of women – for yourself. But you were here on Monday, that's fact, and you didn't tell me about it later.'

'I didn't have a chance, Johnny. You did all the talking. And I'd only been up to see an editor.'

'Who else would pinch the necklace?'

'Johnny, you're angry. I swear this is all in your imagination!'

Reynolds said aside to Gently: 'Johnson places Merryn for us as spying on her on Sunday. The maid places her here on Monday. Then the way she's behaved. It keeps adding up.'

'What about the necklace.'

'Why shouldn't she have pinched it?'

'Too clever.'

'I don't know. Killing people is emotional. You wouldn't be clever all the time.'

'The killer and the thief may be two people.'

'Not likely, Chief. Too improbable.'

'The necklace bothers me. So does the row. We may have been letting the row steal the show. Perhaps the motive is elsewhere. Maybe that's what's so puzzling.'

A cry from Mrs Bannister interrupted them. She had come to to find herself on the settee. The first thing her eyes had rested on had been the stains and she was squirming away from them with an expression of horror.

'You did this deliberately, Superintendent!'

She pushed the policewomen aside and got up from the settee. Indignation brought colour surging back into her cheeks. She quivered, and her dark eyes flashed.

'It was a low trick. You put me there deliberately to see what effect it would have on my nerves. You have descended to this. You are so incompetent you have sunk to trying to scare confessions out of people. But it won't work, Superintendent. All this pantomime is to no purpose. You are fundamentally a very stupid man. You had better have left things to Inspector Reynolds.'

Brenda Merryn clapped. 'Isn't she fabulous? And she knits barbed wire and chews nails.'

'Belt up, Sybil,' Fazakerly said. 'You cackle around like a wet hen.'

Mrs Bannister ignored them. Now she'd seen Sarah Johnson standing rigidly by the window. Her indignation leaked from her and her eyes hooded and softened.

'Beryl!' she exclaimed thrillingly.

'Don't talk to me,' Sarah Johnson said.

'Beryl, look at me. It's been so long.'

'I want nothing to do with you, Mrs Bannister.'

'Beryl, I have a debt. I owe you so much. Now I've found you I want to pay it.'

'Mrs Bannister—'

'Sybil.'

'All I want is to forget you. And the shame I feel. Please don't say any more.'

'Ah, you haven't forgiven me,' Mrs Bannister said, edging closer to the window. 'I've suffered too, Beryl, so much, you'll never know the pain I've endured because of you. I wronged you terribly. Yes, I know it. I should have stood by you come what may. It would have been best. You can never understand what a moment's weakness cost me.'

'I don't want to talk about it.'

'You are bitter, Beryl. Perhaps I don't deserve the

right to repay. But I shall repay, yes, two for one, every bitter moment I've caused you. Come back to me, Beryl. Live with me again. You shall have a flat here if you want it. I'll divide my foolish money with you and we'll live together like two queens. Give me that happiness. To repay. I've suffered enough to deserve it.'

'Are you listening carefully?' Fazakerly said. 'It's a fair offer, Sybil's bint. There's money in it. Sybil's loaded. You'll scarcely get a higher bid.'

'Johnny. Please don't talk like that.'

'Sorry. Of course you must save your face.'

'You're brutal, Johnny.'

'I'm punch-drunk. But Sybil's nice. Love Sybil.'

Sarah Johnson closed her eyes and tears brimmed over and down her cheeks. She ran to the far end of the lounge and threw herself in a chair.

'Touching,' Fazakerly said. 'So touching. You press the button, you get the response. To her, Sybil.'

Mrs Bannister stalked up to him. For a moment it seemed she would strike him a blow. But immediately his hands shaped a boxing defence and he balanced himself on his toes. She turned malignantly to Reynolds.

'You want to know who killed Clytemnestra! It's simple. You need only know one fact and that is that he and his sister-in-law are conspirators. That's the secret. They are in it together. When you know that, you know all.'

'Ha, ha,' Fazakerly said.

'Oh, of course he'll laugh,' Mrs Bannister said. 'They have kept it concealed with very great care, but they could not conceal it from me. She's been his woman all along. She's always been envious of Clytemnestra. The difficulty was how to replace her without saying goodbye to her money. And this was the plot. She was to be killed apparently in a row over poor Beryl, but with so many doubtful circumstances that Siggy would get off. He had this relative in the Yard, please remember, to come interfering on his behalf.'

'Sybil, you're slipping,' Fazakerly said. 'I used to admire your turn for fiction.'

Reynolds gave Gently an embarrassed look. 'Have you any evidence of this, Mrs Bannister?' he asked.

'Plenty of evidence. You heard Beryl say how Merryn went to check her identity. That could only be to tell Clytemnestra to put Clytemnestra into a rage.'

'But did it matter if she were really Beryl Rogers? For the purpose of telling Mrs Fazakerly?'

'Check,' Fazakerly said. 'Check. Take your time, Sybil. You're punching air.'

'It did matter! It gave verisimilitude. It was a truth and not a lie. Clytemnestra could check it if she wanted: her husband was really pursuing Beryl.'

Reynolds looked doubtful. 'It doesn't seem to prove anything, Mrs Bannister.'

'Sybil,' Brenda Merryn said, 'you've had a shock. You're not your old ingenious self.'

Mrs Bannister scythed her with a glance. 'This woman is a psychopathic liar,' she said. 'She is unhinged, as her behaviour has shown, and she has delusions to match her effrontery. Believe nothing she says without proof. She will doubtless deny having been here on Monday.'

'That's my Sybil,' Brenda Merryn said. 'And I could deny it if I wanted.'

'You were seen.' The dark eyes flickered. 'Deny it if you will. You won't be believed.'

'Oh, but I wasn't seen.'

Mrs Bannister nodded. 'Didn't I tell you? A compulsive liar. You have only to allege against her the most obvious of truths and she will start up with a denial.'

'You didn't see me here, Sybil.'

'I have never claimed to. But you were seen.'

'Yet you are the only person who could have seen me.'

'Oh no. That is your blunder.'

'Who did see me then?'

'Albertine.'

Brenda Merryn laughed. 'It was her day off. She wouldn't have been within a mile of the place. You're too handy at finding her jobs, Sybil.'

'Yes,' Mrs Bannister said, 'that may be, Merryn. But on Monday afternoon she came back here. You were unlucky, weren't you? It was very unlikely. But back here she came. And she saw you.'

'Oh Mademoiselle, I am sorry!' Albertine burst out. 'I did not mean any harm to you. It is to help Mr Johnny, this understand. I am sorry, so sorry.'

Brenda Merryn gazed at her. For once she seemed nonplussed. She turned to catch Gently's eye.

'George,' she said. 'There's something funny about this and I'm not certain what it is.'

'Mademoiselle, you were here,' Albertine wailed.

'Yes. But where was it you saw me?'

'It is when I am on the landing downstairs, Mademoiselle. I see you through the doors, going up.'

'You were on the landing outside Madame's flat.'

'Yes, Mademoiselle. It is true.'

Brenda Merryn shook her head. 'That's just the point. It isn't true. You didn't see me.'

'She's lying, of course,' Mrs Bannister sneered. 'Why wouldn't she lie in this situation? It is her word against Albertine's; but I assure you Albertine is commonly truthful.'

'Yes, but I can prove it,' Brenda Merryn said. 'Or rather, you can prove it for me, Sybil. Because though you didn't see me on Monday I saw you. I was careful to check I wasn't seen from your landing.'

'You would not have seen me on the landing.'

Brenda Merryn nodded. 'And what you were doing.'

'Well?'

'You were feeding crumbs from the table to the goldfish in the illuminated basin. And you were alone.'

Mrs Bannister's eyes flicked wider. 'I . . . yes, I did feed the goldfish.'

'Alone.'

'Yes. I was alone.'

'Which is what is so funny,' Brenda Merryn said. 'Albertine didn't see me. You didn't see me. I'll take my oath nobody else saw me. Yet Albertine knew I was here.

'Albertine . . .'

Mrs Bannister turned sharply. Albertine's hand had flown to her mouth. The staring look she'd had on the ledge had come again into her eyes.

'But if she didn't see me, and still knew, then she must have heard me,' Brenda Merryn said. 'And she couldn't have heard me from below, so she must have been up here. Mustn't she?'

Albertine whimpered. It was the only sound to be heard in the lounge which, in spite of the labouring Belling, seemed of a sudden extra chilly. Everyone looked at her. She stood shaking, her hand still near her mouth, her eyes rolling like an idiot's, her bosom heaving silently. She made no effort to say anything. The little whimper was all. She stood defenceless and as it were naked, under the weight of their eyes. Then Mrs Bannister snapped something in French. And Albertine began blurting her head off.

She was using French, and it was much too fast and idiomatic for Gently to follow. She had fallen on her knees before Mrs Bannister and was passionately wringing her hands as the words poured from her. Mrs Bannister apparently understood. She interposed short stabbing questions. She was very pale. At one moment she closed her eyes as though in pain.

Gently looked at Reynolds, who was staring furiously, but he only shook his head. Fazakerly however was straining forward and seemed to be gathering a little of what was said. He was frowning and clenching and unclenching his fists. At last he flung himself on the settee.

'The poor bloody bitch!' he exclaimed. 'No, no, you can't send the poor whore up for that.'

'For what?' Gently said.

'Sybil'll tell you. Oh hell. It breaks your heart.'

He sat punching his fists together and scowling at the carpet.

Albertine finished. She sank on the floor, moaning and giving little shudders. Mrs Bannister, her face white, found a chair and sat. She looked pitifully at Gently.

'Did you understand?' she asked.

'No.'

'I suppose I must tell you. Though it isn't very pretty.'

'I understood,' Brenda Merryn said. 'If you like I'll tell him, Sybil.'

Mrs Bannister looked at Brenda Merryn. Her hand lifted and fell.

'I think I've got it right,' Brenda Merryn said. 'Albertine had a weakness for jewellery, isn't that so?'

Mrs Bannister nodded. 'She sometimes borrows it. She doesn't steal it, it always comes back.'

'She knew Clytie was lunching with you on Monday and that Clytie never locked her door, so she made an excuse to her friend and slipped back to borrow some ear-rings for a dance they were going to. Then she saw the necklace and thought she'd have that. But Clytie came back and she had to hide. She had to stay there while I was with Clytie and until after the row, when Siggy had left. Then she tried to slip out and Clytie caught her. Clytie knew about Albertine's weakness. She made Albertine turn out her bag and there were the necklace and the ear-rings. She threatened Albertine; either Albertine did what she wanted, or Clytie would have her arrested. She forced Albertine down on the settee with her. Albertine saw the pin. She got it. She hit Clytie.'

'I couldn't stand her dirty tricks,' Albertine wailed. 'I am decent, Monsieur. I pulled down the little silver rolling-pin and I made her a good woman.'

Brenda Merryn nodded. 'That's about it. She made Clytie a good woman.'

Half-an-hour later they had everything: the ear-rings, also recovered from the dustbin; a dress, blood-spotted on the front and sleeves; and a pair of blood-spotted gloves. The dress and gloves were found stuffed into a shoe-box and hidden behind Albertine's wardrobe. She had intended putting them in the furnace downstairs but had been prevented by the presence of Dobson. The ear-rings were paste and of small value. Because they were wrapped in tissue Dobson had missed them.

'What'll happen to her?' Fazakerly asked Gently, as they watched Albertine being taken to the lift.

Gently shrugged massively. 'Probably not much. Nobody'll want to throw the book at her.'

'Would it help if I briefed a top counsel.'

'It might help you feel better. It's not necessary.'

'You're a cynical so-and-so, Monsieur.'

'Just answering a question,' Gently grunted.

Fazakerly went. Sarah Johnson went after him,

though he pretended not to notice her. Mrs Bannister, still looking ghostlike, retired into her flat and bolted the door. Brenda Merryn was left. She came up to Gently. They were on the landing outside the Bannister flat. She stood in front of him, looking up, her face slack, her eyes weary.

She gave a little sigh. 'All over, George.'

Gently didn't say anything. Her face was ugly with blotched make-up and there was grime on her chin.

'Is it always like this at the end – just feeling empty and dragged to death?'

'Is that how you feel?'

'Don't you? As though none of it mattered a damn anyway.' She let her head lean to one side. 'But perhaps it's different for you,' she said. 'You see it professionally. It's a job done. You don't let your feelings get involved with it. You're like a surgeon who amputates then washes his hands and goes to tea.'

'Do you know how a surgeon feels?' Gently said.

'No George. Only how I feel. Empty, hopeless and lost. Ready to get on the ledge again. Because that wasn't entirely a fake George, I don't have a lot to keep me here. I didn't before, and I've less now, and I'll be forty next year. Clytie's gone. Siggy. Sybil. And here's the surgeon removing his gloves.'

Her eyes filmed and her mouth trembled. Her blotchy face swam close to his. Then the sharp sound of a slap rang out and she stumbled backwards, holding her cheek.

'You devil! What was that for?'

Gently smiled at her. 'Surgery.'

'My God, you're brutal!'

'Did you say your car was here? We left mine at the station.'

They went down together in the lift. Reynolds had drawn off the reporters in his departing. Bland Street was empty again; nothing of the tumult remained except a coil of rope lying by the steps.

Brenda Merryn unlocked the 1100 and they climbed in. Gently opened the glove-box. It contained no letter. Brenda Merryn looked straight ahead and started the engine and waited.

'Where to?'

'Somewhere quiet for lunch.'

She trilled the engine once or twice.

'And after that?'

'I work for a living. And you'll make your apologies and take the evening surgery.'

'And after that?'

'When do you finish?'

'This is Friday. Say seven.'

'I'll pick you up for a bite in town. Will that do?'

She sighed. 'Perhaps.'

CHAPTER THIRTEEN

HE MET FAZAKERLY again a week later, when he accepted an invitation from him to lunch. It was at the Coq d'Or. It was a very good lunch though it may be less good than the prices on the menu would have led one to expect. Fazakerly was thoughtful. He had been at the Magistrate's hearing and had undertaken to pay for Albertine's defence. He had since had a session with her counsel which had not entirely convinced him she would get off with a light sentence. He wanted to talk about it and to extract a favourable opinion from Gently.

They went into a lounge for their coffee. It was not the lounge where they had met on the previous occasion but a smaller and more intimate room with deep chairs and low tables. The walls were decorated with maroon panels with a golden cock in the centre of each and the full-length velvet curtains were embroidered with cocks in gold wire near the foot. Coffee was served scalding hot. Fazakerly ordered cigars. For some minutes they sat comfortably sipping and smoking and lulled by the soft buzz of conversation.

Fazakerly said: 'You know, I was right in coming to you, even though you wouldn't believe I was innocent. I knew my man. I was a bit of a tick, but I was sure if I involved you in it I would come through. I was innocent, and it had to show up. All I needed was a grain of scepticism.'

'I wasn't necessary,' Gently said. 'Reynolds would have got there just the same. Albertine would have seen to that. Perhaps I saved you the unpleasantness of being charged.'

'For which I'm properly grateful, Monsieur. On reflection, I don't think prison life would have suited me. One gets these notions at odd times but they don't seem to bear the light of day.'

'What are you proposing to do?' Gently asked.

'First, see Albertine off the hook. And what I haven't told you is I have a partner in it. Sybil. Does that surprise you?'

'Not really.'

'No, it wouldn't. You have an eye for tattered humanity. Well, she's going halves in the expense. She'd have probably paid the lot.'

'And after the trial?'

'A long holiday. I think I'm dragged with too many women. I want to cut free of them for one while until my perspective returns.'

Gently sipped his coffee. 'What about Sarah Johnson.'

Fazakerly tilted a shoulder. 'Nothing about her.'

'She loves you.'

'Possibly. The love of a woman.'

'What else can she offer?'

'That's the point.'

He puffed his cigar and looked quizzically at Gently.

'Monsieur is a bachelor,' he said. 'Let him listen to Benedick the Married Man while he imparts true wisdom. A woman's love isn't for you. A woman's love isn't for marriage. A woman's love isn't even directed to biological ends. A woman's love is for herself. She's a hard core of primitive egoism elegantly dressed in hypocrisy, and unless you remember that hard core she'll always be a mystery to you.'

Gently smiled. 'Perhaps you need that holiday.'

'Oh I need it. I'm pretty sour. Just now I'm all for the Greek attitude to women: a slave at home and a whore abroad.'

'Second-class citizens.'

'Even lower. They're distant a thousand incarnations.'

'It may be because of that they need men.'

'Yes. To eat. They live off us.'

He puffed the cigar hard, making a heavy cloud between them. His mouth had a bitter set and his eyes were small and remote.

'Where will you go?' Gently said.

Fazakerly's face relaxed. 'Everywhere. There's a Hillyard twelve-tonner I've got my eye on. She'll do. She's my hand.'

'You'll go sailing?'

'What else? It's the one antidote to illusion. When

your world goes awry there's always a yacht and sea to sail her on. Each time you putter out into the estuary you're starting the Grand Voyage. It may be only to the Point. It may be over the edge of the world.'

'Alone.'

'Alone. If that's what you call it. But one isn't really alone, you know. You're lonelier here in this damned city than you'll ever be with a sheet in your hand.'

'I thought you might take Sarah Johnson with you.'

'By God, you'll never understand.'

'The trial won't be for three months yet. Give me a ring before you set sail.'

Fazakerly shook his head. Gently finished his coffee, stubbed his cigar and went.

Brenda Merryn's opinion had been that Sarah Johnson would be back in favour within a fortnight.

Albertine's trial was interesting. She had been charged with murder committed in the course of a felony, but her counsel submitted that the killing and the (without prejudice) felony constituted separate acts. This was accepted. Counsel then submitted that the killing was justifiable homicide and that the (without prejudice) felony was supposititious and incapable of proof. The first contention was accepted. The felony remained on the indictment. She was found guilty, but her sentence was commuted to deportation and she was returned to her own country. Though perhaps not to Illiers.

Norwich, 1964/5